THE FIEND OF TURLIN'S WELL

Author:
Skeeter Green

Editor:
Jeff Harkness

Layout:
Suzy Moseby

Front Cover Art:
Brian LeBlanc

Interior Art:
Brett Barkley, Brian LeBlanc, Santa Norvaisaite

Cartography:
Robert Altbauer

Swords & Wizardry Conversion:
Jeff Harkness

Virtual Tabletop Developer:
Michael Potter

Frog God Games is:

Bill Webb, Matt Finch, Zach Glazar, Edwin Nagy, Mike Badolato, and John Barnhouse

FROG GOD GAMES

ADVENTURES WORTH WINNING

FROG GOD GAMES
ISBN: 978-1-6656-0158-0
SW PoD

TABLE OF CONTENTS

THE FIEND OF TURLIN'S WELL

By Skeeter Green

A Swords & Wizardry adventure designed for four to six characters of 2nd to 3rd level

Content Warning: Prospective readers should be aware that this is a psychological horror adventure in a swords & sorcery setting. It contains numerous gory descriptions and situations that go beyond the ordinary style of swords & sorcery fiction and are more what one would expect in horror fiction. There is a dark element in most sword & sorcery fiction, which we embrace as a part of that literary genre, but *The Fiend of Turlin's Well* unquestionably crosses over from the swords & sorcery approach of "dark by implication" into the horror genre of "look into the dark." Many of our fans have asked for adventures like this one, but by the same token we don't want to surprise or ambush fans who expect a pure swords & sorcery genre adventure.

INTRODUCTION

This adventure is designed for 4–6 characters of 2nd to 3rd level. The more characters involved in the adventure, the lower the overall character level required for success. As always, you can adjust the adventure as best suits your gaming needs. The adventure takes place in Turlin's Well, an important district in the city of Bard's Gate. Over the course of 10 days, the party encounters a rash of civic disturbances perpetrated by Torad Yarog, a doppelganger posing as one Lassiter D'Torrance, a merchant whom the doppelganger recently killed.

This adventure is designed to be played with mature themes of fear, terror, and psychological manipulation by the villain, so be aware that it could cause problems for some players; it is designed to be easily "dialed down" to whatever level of horror works best for your group of players.

The atmosphere and pacing are more in line with suspense/thriller and horror films than standard fantasy fare. Think more Stephen King than J.R.R. Tolkien; more Jordan Peele than Peter Jackson. If you are unfamiliar with this sort of genre, some media influences to showcase the proper feel are the films *It*, *The Silence of the Lambs*, *Split*, *Us*, and *The Shining*, and directors M. Night Shyamalan, David Fincher, and John Carpenter. The final act in Gaunt House is inspired by Ari Aster, Rob Zombie, and Tobe Hooper.

Again, feel free to adjust the depiction of fright to an appropriate level. The author is a fan of scary and suspenseful movies but understands this is not for everyone. We want you to enjoy the adventure and have some fun!

ADVENTURE SUMMARY

This adventure begins with the characters caught in an upheaval in the district known as Turlin's Well, and later becoming aware of a local vandal known as "The Fiend" stirring up trouble. The Fiend is an individual with a complex background by the name of Torad Yarog. He is also a doppelganger with multiple personalities and the captain of an interdimensional ship called *The Shifting Fortune* that is currently docked in the city's port. Torad left his ship to run ordinary errands on shore, being at that time controlled by a personality he calls "the Captain." However, while he was away, a stressful event caused the personality he calls "The Fiend" to take over. The Fiend cares for little other than slaughter and mayhem, and lost contact with the crew of *The Shifting Fortune*. The ship is more completely described in the adventure *Death-Ship of the Roach Princess*.

Death-Ship of the Roach Princess may be played before or after *The Fiend of Turlin's Well*. If *Death-Ship of the Roach Princess* is not used first, then the clues in *The Fiend of Turlin's Well* lead the characters to *The Shifting Fortune*, the site of the other adventure.

The Demon-Princess Teratashia owns *The Shifting Fortune*, and its crew (including Torad Yarog) are cultists in her service. The ship sent a team of crew members to find their captain and bring him back — they know of his shifting personalities — but they haven't found him yet. In the course of their search, however, one of the cultists dropped a holy symbol of the demon-princess, which a beggar found in the street.

The adventure begins when the characters encounter the beggar (see **Adventure Start**).

The Fiend progresses from simple vandalism to assault, and eventually to murder, leading the characters on a series of encounters, all the while orchestrating the entire affair. His violence targets a wererat clan based in Turlin's Well known as the Pipers for more attention and to provoke retaliation. While most of the city's guardsmen consider this "criminal vs. criminal" retaliation and initially downplay it, a few begin to pay attention to the details of the crimes and their rapid escalation.

After the characters get involved, the Fiend begins performing increasingly violent acts and atrocities, staging events to lure the characters into tracking him down. Early in the investigation of these displays, it should become clear to at least one member of the party that the Fiend *wants* them to find him. They are playing a game, although the rules and objective are not yet clear. The characters have several opportunities to inquire with guardsmen and the city watch about the crimes, although most investigations produce only more questions or wild rumors. Eventually, the characters confront the Fiend in a rundown estate known as Gaunt House.

The Fiend of Turlin's Well take places a few weeks after the events detailed in *A Matter of Faith* from **Bard's Gate** (published by **Frog God Games**). That adventure is not needed to play this one, although it gives a richer backstory to current events. Some familiarity with Bard's Gate, and that adventure specifically, makes running the encounters in this adventure easier.

BARD'S G
1 SQUARE = 220 FT
W N S E
Landwehr Lane
Pokorny Ave.
Easley Way
Metcalf Ave.
Stephens Ave.
Circle of Gargoyles
Turlin's Well
West Sardinha Way
Reyst Way
Adam's Ave.
Plaza of Dark Pleasures
Canal
East

Background

Torad Yarog is a doppelganger, a cultist of the Demon-Princess Teratashia, and has an extremely unstable mind comprising multiple personalities. He is also the captain of a demonic ship known as *The Shifting Fortune* that has docked in the city to gather information for Teratashia and to plant seeds of chaos. Torad went ashore two weeks ago to meet with another of Teratashia's agents in the city, a cultist by the name of Lassiter D'Torrance. They quarreled, and in the stress of the moment, Torad Yarog shifted from his "Captain" persona into his "Fiend" persona. The result was fatal for Lassiter D'Torrance. In the time afterward, the Fiend has been living in D'Torrance's house and posing as the man when necessary. Torad Yarog's crew do not know anything about Lassiter D'Torrance; the agent's existence was known only to Torad Yarog. The crew of *The Shifting Fortune* thus aren't aware that they should be looking for someone named Lassiter D'Torrance — as far as they know, the captain simply disappeared into thin air. Even though they know their captain is a doppelganger, their search has been thrown off by the fact that they are looking for him in places such as inns and taverns where a stranger might stay rather than in a well-established city dweller's residence. D'Torrance lived in a building known as Gaunt House, which is now the lair of the Fiend, and it is from this place that the doppelganger is perpetrating its growing reign of chaos and terror.

The main link that allows the characters to connect Lassiter D'Torrance and Gaunt House to the Fiend is that D'Torrance worked as an agent for the criminal Wheelwrights Guild. The Wheelwrights deal in information, which made them the perfect association for an information-gathering cultist such as D'Torrance. As it is established in this adventure, the link is not direct; the characters are asked to deal with D'Torrance rather than following a series of clues leading to his location. From their perspective, they stumble upon the solution rather than puzzling it out. This is deliberate; the pacing of a "mystery-type" adventure is usually very slow, whereas the accidental discovery of a horrible lair allows for a much faster-paced and movie-like progression of events.

How to Use This Adventure

This adventure is investigation-based and does not necessarily follow a linear path. As such, important encounters are detailed, and a rough timeline is provided when important events happen over the course of 10 days in the city.

You are strongly encouraged to read the entire adventure, the various sidebars throughout, and *The Lyre Valley Beholder* (see **Appendix E: The Lyre Valley Beholder**) to gather all the clues, bits of evidence, information, hints, and suggestions to make the adventure flow properly for your campaign. Your own notes and suggestions help integrate the players into the story; the author is providing a framework for how these events unfold, but to truly have the players invested in the outcome, you should personalize this and make it your own.

Not all the encounters are necessary for play, and more than enough are provided to keep the narrative moving. You may pick any of the encounters to discard, although certain encounters are helpful to build tension and advance the investigation. Again, read through the entire adventure and find the bits that work for your group. If you have your own ideas that follow the theme, by all means, incorporate them!

Magic is of limited use in the investigation; something is blocking magical investigations into the perpetrator (the fact that he is of extraplanar origin and still tied in arcane fashion to *The Shifting Fortune*). The city claims all available resources are being poured into the investigation. If something is not done soon, dire circumstances may befall the legacy of the city.

The encounters provided offer plenty of opportunities for the characters to earn experience points toward advancement, but if you choose to run a milestone-based progression, several "set breaks" provide good points for advancement. The characters should be 3rd level, or very close, by the time they enter Gaunt House.

Cinematic Gameplay

This adventure is written with the concept of "cinematic elements," an attempt to replicate the feelings of watching a psychological thriller, a horror movie, or a suspense film. Customizing this adventure for your group is imperative for the story to work. Reading through the adventure first as a "movie summary" may be helpful in play.

The initial act of the adventure (if you're thinking of it as a suspense movie) is primarily background information and setup, which then leads to more encounters where the Fiend gets closer to the party, and ends with a final confrontation.

The Fiend

The characters encounter the Fiend multiple times during the early part of the adventure, although he is content to watch them … for now. Use the following information as needed if the characters somehow uncover his identity.

The Fiend in its natural form is seven feet tall with wiry muscles, stretched skin, and a lean torso. At first glance, the creature appears like a classic gargoyle: short, curved horns, a fanged mouth, wicked claws, and pupil-less eyes. It does not show any wings, and its legs are exaggerated, almost like a frog's. It gives the impression of a runner, and the legs end in massive paw-like talons.

The Fiend is a doppelganger, and in its persona as the Fiend, it is a psychopathic killer with no regard for decency. The Fiend suffers from a malady known as fractured mind syndrome, with the Fiend being just one of eight personalities inhabiting the doppelganger (see **Madness: Fractured Mind Syndrome** below).

Torad Yarog, The Fiend, Doppelganger: HD 6; **HP** 41; **AC** 5[14]; **Atk** claws (1d12); **Move** 9; **Save** 11 (5 vs. magic); **CL/XP** 8/800; **Special:** fractured mind syndrome, immune to sleep and charm, mimic shape, save 5 vs. magic, spells (MU 2/1). (***Monstrosities*** 129)

Spells: 1st—*charm person*, *magic missile*; 2nd—*phantasmal force*.

Equipment: envoy's signet (see **Appendix B**), packet of *dust of disappearance*, *potion of gaseous form*, *potion of extra healing*.

Madness: Fractured Mind Syndrome

The fractured mind malady is a terrible neurosis in which the afflicted host's personality becomes dissociated, or split, into two or more distinctly different parts. In some cases, these differing personalities vie for control of the host, excluding the other parts. If a particularly dominant state assumes control for a long period of time, the other parts may suffer from their ongoing submission.

Each of the parts of the host's personality, or states, tries to assert dominance in the host body to control movement, emotions, and responses to outside stimuli. While these states can and do frequently work together to survive, often a more dominant state emerges and influences, or outright controls, the others.

This madness is barely understood and difficult to treat without magical intervention. Even with magical aid, the inner workings of the mind are tricky to alter; as much damage can be done attempting to "cure" the host as what they are currently suffering.

A host suffering from an acute case of fractured mind syndrome *becomes* the state in control. Severe cases of the disorder speak languages unknown to the host, display advanced spellcraft practiced by previously untrained common folk, exhibit feats of inhuman strength by "normal" looking commoners, and other such extreme changes.

Getting Started

The story starts the characters out in the Turlin's Well District of Bard's Gate. They could become involved in the events in several ways:

- The characters are from Bard's Gate, know someone from Bard's Gate who asks for their help with vandals, or they are traveling through Bard's Gate, pick up a copy of *The Lyre Valley Beholder* to read, and are intrigued by the headlines.
- The party, or a single character, is part of a secret organization or guild of Bard's Gate and is tasked by a superior to investigate the events.
- The characters are in town trying to relax and get caught up in the district's tension.
- If the characters played through *A Matter of Faith*, they may already fill one or more of these roles.

Bard's Gate Locals: If the characters are based in Bard's Gate, you can assume they know about the "local troubles" in the Turlin's Well District. Graffiti and vandalism are on the rise, but authorities are shrugging it off as growing pains — and some of the instances are nothing more than that. They do not initially take the matters seriously. Some small businesses are tired of the senseless malice and are raising their own funds to hire private security — adventurers or mercenaries — to look after their interests (and to hunt the miscreants responsible). *The Lyre Valley Beholder* is running some stories about the incidents but is not providing much in-depth coverage. It reports that the vandalism has been growing in intensity for the last few weeks since the "clown kidnappings" but it does not provide many details.

If the characters played through the adventure *A Matter of Faith*, they have access to all the contacts they made in that adventure and may be able to gather additional information before starting, at your discretion.

Secret Organization: Another way to get the characters involved is to have them start out as new agents in one of Bard's Gate's many guilds or secret organizations. The details of these are best left up to your campaign, but some suggestions are:

- Operatives seeking to prove themselves to the Greycloaks are tasked with investigating the vandalism, determining if it's a local district problem, and deciding if a larger issue exists. When they can provide verifiable information (evidence) of a larger issue to leadership, they get the authority to investigate further.
- Characters working with the Sisters of Maiden's Cross (perhaps repaying a favor granted in *A Matter of Faith*) are supporting that group's patrols in the district, attempting to root out more of the slaver's network. When the party experiences the assault, the sisters are initially not interested. However, after three days in seclusion, they ask the party to investigate the wererats.
- Characters interested in joining the Saints of Turlin's Well are asked to find out who is responsible for the district's unrest and graffiti, as well as investigating the wererat nests just to keep tabs on their activities. Common sense says the wererats are either involved or know who is involved. The characters' Saints' contact offhandedly mentions consulting the Beggars Guild but says no more on the subject.
- If the characters are somehow connected to the Underguild (through affiliations with the Wheelwrights, the Shadow Masks, or the Red Blades) or the Beggars Guild, you can tailor what information you pass along to the party. It should be in line with information gathered from other sources, but may be more direct, as the shadier guilds already have an eye on the vandal in the Well; they just don't stop him. The Beggars Guild is concerned about their missing members, and they take drastic actions on Day 8 to get the city's attention.

We just want a break! If the characters are in Bard's Gate "between adventures" or heading out to their first dungeon crawl, they may be unintentionally swept up in the chaos when the Fiend strikes. The Well Watch does not initially link the troubles together until the fourth evening when they receive a very blatant piece of evidence.

Adventure Start

The beggar is **Yourn Keelo**, who has just found an unholy symbol of the Demon-Princess Teratashia in the alleyway where it was dropped by the cultist-crewmembers of *The Shifting Fortune* who are now on shore looking for their missing captain, Torad Yarog (the Fiend). Yourn knows that if a beggar like himself shows up at a jeweler or a pawnbroker with a solid gold holy symbol — he does not know it is demonic — he will immediately be suspected of theft. Thus, he is willing to sell the object for only 10 gp when it is obviously worth 50 gp at the very least.

The characters do not need to enter the alley to talk with Yourn, but if they do, they notice only one other beggar sitting at the end of the alley where it joins with another street. This second beggar watches the proceedings without much interest and does not appear as if he will interfere at all. However, this second beggar is actually Torad Yarog, the **Fiend**. Torad is paying very close attention indeed, for the characters interrupted him only a few moments from killing Yourn. Now that they have gotten involved, however, he does not reveal himself and simply watches and waits.

Yourn Keelo, Male Human Commoner: HP 3; AC 9[10]; **Atk** club (1d6); **Move** 12; **Save** 18; **AL** N; **CL/XP** B/10; **Special:** none. (*Monstrosities* 254)

Any character with a religious background is able to tell that the holy symbol is demonic in nature, although it still is worth 50 gp. It is not magical. The character might be able to identify that the symbol is specifically that of the Demon-Princess Teratashia, in which case they would know some or all of the information in **Appendix D: Teratashia**.

Whether or not the characters purchase the holy symbol from Yourn, the encounter sets two things in motion. First, Yourn is doomed. The characters might hear the next day that he died in a rather abominable fashion with his eyes removed. Secondly, the Fiend knows that the characters are aware of the existence of the holy symbol, and this draws his attention to them.

FEATURES OF THE TURLIN'S WELL DISTRICT

Character: "The Well," as Turlin's Well is usually called by the locals, is described by some as a rough-and-tumble gathering place of wayward adventuring types and low-rent charlatans. While in some instances this may be true, the Council of Burghers knows the Well to be the most thriving district in the city. Large amounts of adventuring coin are still spent in the shops and taverns, and while licenses for new businesses have slowed, the booming shipyards more than make up for the loss of new revenue. The boom of Turlin's Well has been so successful, and consistent, that the council has spread its prosperity to the Outer District and the East Docks, reinvigorating them as well.

Businesses: Taverns, inns, craft shops, and shops catering to adventurers are located here. Most shops are also residences, with 65% of the structures dedicated to private housing.

Prices: Prices in the Well District are 15%–20% above standard due to swelling taxes resulting from the expanded growth of new and successful businesses here.

Building Type: Structures in the Well District are mostly brick-and-wood, two-story buildings that are plaster or stucco coated in a clean, pleasant white. Many businesses have a fine mural painted on the side of their building in fresco to show the sort of operation that they run. Several buildings are also tagged in graffiti, a growing problem in the district.

Guard Details: The Well Watch is a good-natured band of about 80 individuals. The group consists of patrols of 4–6 members and may be encountered once every 20–30 minutes — when they aren't busy hanging out in the local taverns while on duty. Some groups contain low-level adventurers looking to make an extra buck. The Well Watch had a reputation for being easily "distracted" — bribed — but that changed after the events described in *A Matter of Faith*.

RUMORS

During *The Fiend of Turlin's Well*, rumors and information gathered from locals are critical in the characters' investigations. As with all rumors, some are factual, some are red herrings, and some are a mixture of both. It takes a concerted effort from the characters (and the players) to sift fact from fiction. You are encouraged to tailor these rumors as necessary based on the deductive skills of your players. Help them if needed, but encourage them to follow clues and see where the leads take them.

Rumors are discovered by spending one hour asking around and spending 5 sp. This allows a character to roll once on the **Rumors in The Well** table. Spending more money typically doesn't give any better information. The characters have three opportunities to find out rumors each day (morning, afternoon, and evening checks).

Specific groups might offer better (or in some cases, worse) information; interrogating a beggar adds +5 to the roll and costs an extra 5 sp; asking the guards of the local district costs an extra 1 gp, but gives no bonus to the roll; and if the characters manage to consult a wererat nest in the Well, it costs a flat 10 gp, but you can choose what rumor they hear (for good or ill). Feel free to provide a different rumor if they reroll one they've already heard.

1d20	Rumor
1	"Nope, haven't heard much lately. Saw something about vandals in the *Beholder*, but don't know nuthin' beyond that. Sorry."
2	"Eh? Vandals? Yeah, saw some folks paintin' buildings on the south end, but jus' figured they was upgradin'."
3–4	"Trouble in the Well again? Boy, that place is cursed or somethin'. Seems like every couple o' months, more trouble. I ain' heard nothing though."
5	"It's them damnable Huuns! They laid a curse on the city when they was here!"
6–7	"The city has rats. Big ones. As big as people … an' walk like 'em, too. 'Specially down at the docks in the Well."
8	"Beggars come and go, but sure seems like there be less of 'em 'round the Well lately."
9–10	"Seen the watch fish a body outta the East canal, under the Reyst Way bridge. Was pretty smashed up, an' the current sure di'n't do that."
11	"Utello's always been a weird bastard. Anybody whose art is that screwy can't be right in the head."
12	"Yeah, been pretty tense in the district lately. Heh, wouldn't take much to set these people on their heads, now."
13	"Seems like the southern district is getting hit the hardest lately."
14	"Heard some talk in the bar last night. Them brotherhood gangers are gonna clip some heads, I think."
15	"Personally, and you didn't hear this from me, but I think the Wheels are behind it all, making their move in the district."
16	"You think that Fiend guy is a real artist? I mean, I know it's vandalism, and it's gross, but something about it is just so …"
17	"Gaunt House has always been creepy as Hell. Maybe the squatters there know something?"
18	"What if this is just a ploy by the guilds to keep everybody all stirred up so that we can't get back to normal from what the clown did?"
19	"The guard don't take none of our worries seriously. Maybe it's them causing all the trouble?"
20+	"You *never* see a watchman walkin' alone in the Well. They ain't tough enough. But I seen one walkin' around last few nights, 'long the south side of East canal, across o' Founder's Park."

EVENT TIMELINE

Because this adventure is not a linear dungeon crawl, the characters may discover information, evidence, and clues in a haphazard order. As keeping track of information may become a chore, a timeline of events is provided to manage a consistent flow and to keep the players from getting confused about what their characters know.

Manesdag, Sistersdag, et al., are the names of the days of the week in the Lost Lands. Freyrmond is the month during which this take place (roughly March). For more information about keeping time in the Lost Lands, please consult **The World of the Lost Lands** campaign setting from **Frog God Games**. The events in bold type are detailed below the table.

Day	Date	Discovery
1	Manesdag, Freyrmond 5	The characters arrive in town and get settled. They hear the Well District is having some troubles.
2	Sistersdag, Freyrmond 6	Characters are free to do any city tasks.
		Characters encounter the **Crazed Prophet** if walking the district.
3	Thingsdag, Freyrmond 7	Characters are free to do any city tasks.
		If the characters are out at night, or in a tavern, the **Vigilantes** encounter occurs.
4	Solsdag, Freyrmond 8	Characters feel a palpable tension in the community. Passersby do not look characters in the eye, and everyone seems harried. Guards at the shops are grim and jumpy. Shopkeepers are impatient and downright rude.
		The Assault happens at night.
		District sentiment never settles after tonight.
5	Ardsdag, Freyrmond 9	The district is scared. News of **The Assault** spreads through the Well and spills out into the Outer District as well. More vigilante groups are forming.
		The Gruesome Package is discovered.
6	Djinsdag, Freyrmond 10	**Duloth's Outrage** (as the meeting is called in the *Beholder*) occurs just before noon. A riot is threatened, but nothing happens today. Other districts notice the tension and disruption of the Well, and the council calls a guilds meeting to discuss.
7	Mootsdag, Freyrmond 11	The Pipers come out of their burrow to fight. The Sisters act against the wererats. The Fiend gets closer to the characters.
8	Manesdag, Freyrmond 12	The Beggars Guild is tired of being ignored. They start a riot in the Well.
9	Sistersdag, Freyrmond 13	The characters investigate Gaunt House.

Fixed Encounters

These next encounters are automatic, the result of outside events and the Fiend's focus on the characters due to the fact that they have seen the holy symbol.

Crazed Prophet (Day 2)

This encounter takes place anytime on the second day that the characters are in town.

As the characters are out in the district, they hear a street evangelist exhorting the few stragglers on the street to the worship of Jamboor, suggesting "Jamboor loves us all! None are excluded from his embrace!" This specific passage suggests that everyone dies, but followers of Jamboor may seek to hasten the journey. It is a commonly held tenet in the religion but embraced heavily by the darker practitioners of the faith.

Interactions. If the street preacher is questioned about his message or his faith, he begins to babble incoherently, occasionally throwing out such fare as "Jamboor is all things!" and "Throw off the mortal coil! Embrace oblivion!" Continue giving similar nonsensical jargon as needed. When the characters tire of the preacher, he finishes the encounter with "The real strong have no need to prove it to the weak." With that, the preacher falls into a fit of seizures and is unable to communicate further. Characters can determine that the preacher is in no lasting danger from the fit but he will not be able to speak further until he calms down.

After the characters leave, the street prophet (the **Fiend**) recovers, and when no one is looking, he changes shape into an average citizen and walks away to continue his plan.

Clues. A Pinwheel Message. After the characters leave the encounter, have the character with the highest intelligence attempt to roll below his or her intelligence on 3d6. If successful, something in the crazed prophet's rant strikes that character as unusual (more than a regular crazed rant!). Replaying the encounter in their head, the character realizes that no cleric of Jamboor would be without their wheel of insight, even in a crazed state. If the party returns to the location where they encountered the prophet, a pinwheel is on the ground — a highly decorated version they definitely *did not* notice there before. If the characters spin the wheel, the designs on the blades form the words "He is Redeemed" as they spin.

Vigilantes (Day 3)

This encounter takes place after dusk of the third night that the characters are in town.

This is an important encounter for the characters to understand the "vibe" currently in the district. A group of **8 vigilantes** is patrolling the district, and they're looking for trouble. The group is drunk, making this a potentially explosive encounter. **Slack Barley**, their leader, is belligerent and nearly incoherent. If approached, he slurs out that "weel handler this troobl …" If the party attempts to question Barley or the group, he initiates a confrontation.

Slack Barley, Male or Female Human Vigilante Leader:
HP 18; AC 7[12]; Atk longsword (1d8) or dagger (1d4); Move 12; Save 14; AL C; CL/XP 3/60; Special: none. (*Monstrosities* 254)
Equipment: chainmail, longsword, dagger, 1d6 gp.

Vigilantes, Male or Female Human Commoners (6): HP 6, 5x2, 4, 3x2; AC 7[12]; Atk club (1d4) or dagger (1d4); Move 12; Save 17; AL C; CL/XP 1/15; Special: none. (*Monstrosities* 254)
Equipment: leather armor, club, 2 daggers, 2d4 cp.
Note: One of the vigilantes is the **Fiend**. See below for details.

Confrontation. Barley initially spits at the party, calling them outsiders, then moves to accusing them of the problems in the Well, adding in several imaginary embellishments. It's clear he is angry, distraught with the situation, and distrustful of anyone he doesn't know. The rest of the group follows Barley's lead, but if a fight breaks out, they hesitate for one round as they decide if they should get involved. If the characters attack first, however, they are fully invested.

If the characters attempt a civil discourse with the group, Barley calms somewhat. However, he's too drunk for any guile or machismo to sink in. If Barley is calmed, he tells the party that he heard a rumor in "the Guild" (the Aleman's Guild, **Area TW39**) that "dat dirty fiend-folk was comin' out ta'night. 'ere red-eye for 'im!"

Clues. A Rumor. Barley's clue about the Fiend coming out is true. However, unbeknownst to him, one of the vigilantes in his group is the **Fiend** taking the shape of a regular citizen. It does not join the fight against the characters, and instead prefers to hang in the back to get a measure of them. If confronted, it holds up its hands and pleads mercy. It does not want to fight the characters … yet.

If this is the first time the Fiend is meeting the characters, it is intensely interested in them and scrutinizes them openly. Choose a random character and have them make a saving throw to notice the vigilante "giving them the eyeball."

The Assault (Day 4)

This encounter takes place on the fourth night that the party is in town (see the **Event Timeline**).

At some time just after midnight, a high-pitched, chittering scream is heard throughout the southern Well District. Another bloodcurdling wail is let out and after a few seconds is abruptly halted. The ensuing silence is chilling and frightening; not even the local strays utter a sound. It's as if the entire city is holding its breath for fear of discovery.

Setting the Stage. After several minutes, the city resumes its natural evening routine. If the characters move in the general direction of the disturbance, they discover a crowd of people gathered around the freshly painted wall of a shop with a large pile of rags and debris below it. What follows unfolds in tragic slow-motion for the characters …

The first thing characters see is the fresh paint obviously covering an incident of vandalism. The smell of paint is strong, along with a lighter smell of copper and some other tainted, sewage odor …

The next thing the characters are aware of is the design on the wall: It looks like writing, but they are unable to read it clearly due to the milling onlookers, the approaching Well Watch, and the poor lighting conditions. As they move closer through the milling crowd, the message becomes visible:

"NOW I HAVE YOUR ATTENTION" is written in a haphazard, manic script.

The Well Watch investigates the pile of rags at the base of the wall directly under the message. A small, still body is uncovered, barely breathing, and the watch quickly moves to keep the crowd away. They push people back to create a perimeter, which begins to rile and infuriate the crowd. Members of the crowd begin shouting questions such as "Another child?" and "Who is it now?" An animal sense of fear and fury simmers; characters should feel as if this could spark a riot in the district. This is a heinous, shocking act distinctly different from what was previously mundane vandalism. Trouble is escalating in the district and could get out of hand quickly.

If the characters wait until the crowd disperses and ask about the beating, they gather that the watch is keen on keeping the public calm, but not too interested in following up on the incident. Characters can finagle out of one of the guards that the body is a member of the Pipers, a notorious wererat nest in the district. "Likely some kinda gang trouble. We'll get 'em patched up, and send 'im on 'is way."

A Watcher. The **Fiend** is in the crowd, disguised as a normal citizen, watching the authority's reaction. It pays close attention to the characters' reactions, judging their motives. If the characters question the authorities, the Fiend knows he has them hooked.

Clues. Backstory. The scrawling on the wall has a distinct flourish to the style of the letters. It's not local and has an aristocratic flair, despite the effort to make it look hurried. The characters can determine that whoever wrote this is trying to portray madness while acting quite calculated.

Aftermath of the Assault

In the morning, the entire district is buzzing with the incident of the previous night. It seems that gossip and inuendo have traveled on wings of fear; every corner of the district, and the city at large for that matter, can speak of nothing else. Guards patrol the district during daylight hours, in double the usual numbers. Shopkeepers complain about the added patrols driving off customers, at the same time lamenting the sorry condition of the city. Citizens travel in groups when performing their chores or errands; a general distrust seeps into the societal groundwater.

The evening is worse. The Well Watch detachments are augmented by patrols of a **sheriff** and **4 constables**. These roving patrols cover each street every hour, and anyone encountered on the streets after dusk are asked about their business, as well as any personal information the sheriffs can get out of them. At this point, the guards are still civil, if terse, and are doing their best not to frighten the Well inhabitants more than necessary. High Burgess Cylyria has bills posted on each street informing the public that no resource is being spared to apprehend the guilty party. Which all goes for naught …

Sheriff, Male or Female Human (Ftr3): HP 18;
    AC 6[13]; **Atk** longsword (1d4+1) or light crossbow
    (1d4+1); **Move** 12; **Save** 12; **AL** N; **CL/XP** 3/60;
    Special: +1 to hit and damage strength bonus,
    multiple attacks (3) vs. creatures with 1 or fewer HD.
Equipment: leather armor, shield, longsword, light crossbow,
    10 bolts.
Constables, Male or Female Humans (Ftr1) (4): HP 7, 5x2,
    4; **AC** 6[13]; **Atk** longsword (1d8) or light crossbow (1d4+1);
    Move 12; **Save** 14; **AL** N; **CL/XP** 1/15; **Special:** none.
Equipment: leather armor, shield, longsword, light crossbow,
    10 bolts.

The Gruesome Package (Day 5)

On the night after the assault, another body is found in the middle of South Landwehr Lane. The victim's limbs are broken and bent backward behind his back, tied together as if in a morbid gift-wrapping. A note is tucked to the chest of the victim, under a bow in the rope. The note simply says, "I THOUGHT YOU WERE LOOKING?" Under the note, in the victim's clothing, are a set of extracted eyeballs. They are not the victim's.

As the guards begin removing the body, the man regains consciousness and says, "I. Can't. Feel … my arms …" and then passes out. After a few seconds, the body shifts and transforms, transmuting from rat-human hybrid, to human, to giant rat, until finally settling as a small human. A gasp escapes as the body goes limp.

The sheriff takes possession of the deceased, and one of the constables leaves to get a cart to take it away. The constable who leaves to get the cart is the **Fiend**, who is keeping a close watch on the investigation and the characters' involvement. He does not return, and after some time, another constable leaves to retrieve the cart.

Cinematic Element. This encounter should be played out as graphically as you feel your players can handle. This should be shocking and disturbing, and possibly elicit an angry, frustrated, or even desperate response. The characters need to be invested in the killer at this point and eager to hunt him down.

Clues. The Note and the Body. In the time the constables are waiting for the cart to arrive to remove the body, a character may be able to convince the sheriff to allow the party to examine the body. All the victim's limbs are broken in multiple places, and a faint discoloration is evident around the victim's mouth. Something ingested shortly before the brutal attack stained the victim's mouth. If the characters alert the sheriff, he or she offers to inform the party if anything unusual is discovered about the discoloration, which is the residue of a paralytic poison.

Duloth's Outrage (Day 6)

The morning after the grisly discovery, the district erupts. Led by **Guildmaster Duloth Armitage**, a crowd gathers in the Circle of Gargoyles to call out the ineffectual leadership of the high burgess and the council. Insults are thrown, challenges to authority are made, and the crowd is whipped into a frenzy. Threats of rioting and work stoppages are proffered, and Armitage, as leader of the Wheelwrights, promises, "If the council can't keep you safe, maybe it's time for new leadership! The Wheelwrights keep your goods safe, maybe we should keep *you* safe?" This receives thunderous applause from the crowd, and constables and city watchmen move in to break up the gathered crowd before a mob takes shape. The watch maintains control this day, but the pulse of the city is up, and other districts are looking at the situation with new interest.

Guildmaster Duloth Armitage (Ftr7): HP 35; AC 3[16]; **Atk** *+2 dagger* (1d4+3) or *+1 extra attack longsword* x2 (1d8+2) or light crossbow (1d4+1 + poison); **Move** 12; **Save** 6; **AL** C; **CL/XP** 8/800. **Special:** −1[+1] dexterity AC bonus, +1 to hit missile bonus, +1 to hit and damage strength bonus, multiple attacks (7) vs. creatures with 1 or fewer HD, parry −3.

Equipment: *+2 leather armor, +2 dagger, +1 extra attack longsword*, light crossbow, 10 bolts (w/ large spider venom, save at −1 or die), *bag of holding, ring of protection +2*, 3 vials of black lotus extract, several hundred gp in coin and gems.

Day 3 Through Day 6

The End of the Beginning. The next two days are a descent into nightmare for the Well District. Both nights bring a new event, each one more destructive to the city than the last. The characters find some clues during this time and may encounter a disguised Fiend several times. At this point, the city is nearing a breaking point. Small groups begin rioting in the Well and Outer districts but are quickly subdued by watchmen or other gangs. Vigilantism is common from the Lyre Bridge eastward, and innocent citizens are now being dragged into the streets and beaten on suspicion of involvement in the crimes or of harboring the guilty. The bars are packed, even in the light of day, with angry citizens forging plans to "take back their city," no matter the cost.

Behind the Civic Curtain. The city council, the Free Defenders, and even the Lyreguard all watch with a trained eye. They are careful not to intervene yet, as undermining the stability of the Well Watch and the constables could be disastrous for the district. An increased presence of "Lyreguards out and about" on the King's and Lyre's bridges give truth to the situation. The council discusses the day's events every two days and meet nightly beginning on Djinsdag, Freyrmond 10. Duloth Armitage is barred from these proceedings as a reprimand for his speech.

The next three nights push the district and the city into depths from which it will not soon recover. Civic instability in one of the more prosperous districts shakes Bard's Gate to its core. Coming so soon after the tragedy of the slavers, the public's nerves are frayed and their attitudes volatile. Depending on the actions of the characters, they can either greatly improve, or vastly worsen, the plight of the city.

The Night of Day 7

"Let slip the Hounds of Hell, for the Game is Truly Afoot" — Octavio D'Scale

Enough is Enough

This encounter occurs on the seventh night, the evening after Guildmaster Armitage gives his rousing speech. The characters have been looking for clues about the wererat nests — either through their own investigations or with information received from the Sisters. A group of **6 Piper thugs** have come out of the sewers to "get their fur up" and are looking for trouble. When they encounter the well-armed characters, they aren't looking to talk. They attack immediately and offer no quarter.

Piper Thugs, Male and Female Wererats (6): HD 3; HP 20, 17, 15x2, 14, 10; AC 6[13]; **Atk** bite (1d3), short sword (1d6) or light crossbow (1d4+1); **Move** 12; **Save** 14; **AL** C; **CL/XP** 4/120; **Special:** +1 or better magic or silver weapons to hit, control rats, lycanthropy, surprise (1–4 on 1d6). (*Monstrosities* 307)

Equipment: short sword, light crossbow, 10 bolts.

Cinematic Element. This encounter has a probability of incapacitating the characters quickly if they don't have access to magic weapons and spells capable of harming the wererats. Play the encounter out, and if the characters are overwhelmed, they have backup waiting in the wings. This shouldn't be a campaign-ending defeat if the characters are not prepared; it should advance the story narrative as explained below.

The Pipers Win. If the Pipers prove to be too much, they are careful not to kill any of the characters, only to wound them. In addition, they do not bite, attacking only with short swords or light crossbows; they are not trying to infect anyone. When the characters are down, the wererats suddenly shift their attacks to the group of **4 Sisters of the Order of Maiden's Cross paladins** who show up.

The fight is gruesome, with casualties on both sides. If four Pipers are downed, the last two attempt to flee. If the Sisters lose two members and it looks as if the Pipers might win, one of the remaining two Sisters turns on the other! This is the **Fiend** trying to sow chaos and further distrust in the community. When the Fiend turns on the last Sister, the Pipers flee the situation in surprise.

Order of the Maiden's Cross Paladins, Female Paladins of Muir (Pal3) (3): HP 23, 21x2; AC 2[17]; **Atk** *+1 longsword* (1d8+1); **Move** 12; **Save** 10; **AL** L; **CL/XP** 3/60; **Special:** immune to disease, lay on hands, warhorse.

Equipment: plate mail, shield, *+1 longsword, potion of healing*, holy symbol of Muir, 2d4 sp.

Note: The Fiend is posing as one of the Sisters.

The Sisters Save the Day. If the characters have a hard time with the Piper crew but are not being decimated, the Fiend "comes to their rescue." The Sisters show up with their magic weapons and are able to overcome the wererats' immunities. If the Sisters help win the fight, the characters are invited to aid in their "display to the public" and drag the wererats back to Maiden's Cross. The Fiend, disguised as one of the Sisters, does not reveal itself to anyone yet. Its unfamiliarity with Maiden's Cross doctrine and habits allows a suspicious character to roll below his or her wisdom on 4d6 (or 3d6 if they are from Bard's Gate) to note that something is off about that Sister and that she is likely an imposter.

Assuming the party does not indicate that they have discovered the Fiend, it continues its charade and plays along with the carousing for the evening. This particular Sister is unusually engaging with the men in the group. If confronted, the Fiend downplays the interaction and excuses itself. It then flees when out of direct sight.

The Characters Prevail. If the characters handle the Pipers, the Sisters appear after the fight, congratulate the characters on killing the "underground scum," and drag the bodies off to hang them from the roof of Maiden's Cross (**Area TW27**). One of the Sisters pats a female character on the shoulder and says, "Great work. First round's on me!" (She does not make this offer if all the characters appear male.) That Sister is the Fiend keeping tabs on the characters. If they discover the doppelganger, it fights only enough to get away.

Clues. A Scroll. If the characters defeat the Pipers, they find a scroll on one of them that describes a tall, clown-faced human with a strange musical box (the description is of Dropsy the Clown, a main villain in *A Matter of Faith*) that the Pipers are looking for. Dropsy's involvement depends on your campaign; if you have not played through *A Matter of Faith*, or choose not to tie it to this adventure, have the description be of any red herring you choose. The description is to show that the Pipers are looking for someone, but that they have the wrong person.

Day 8

The Beggars Guild finally takes matters in the city into its own hands. The day of Manesdag, Freyrmond 12, the Beggars Guild takes to the streets before dawn and begins commandeering the district.

Synchronized Events. At multiple locations, simultaneously at the sixth hour after midnight, the Beggars create five "civic disturbances":

The northwest end of the bridge near Virthalia's House is blocked and a fire is started in the street.

The south end of the bridge on Los Road near the Golden Palms is blocked by several broken wagons and carts.

The west end of the bridge on Adam's Avenue — near Bard's Gate, too! — is piled high with garbage, debris, and barrels of metal from Volwild's.

The southwest end of the bridge on Reyst Way near the Wyvern's Tail is barricaded and burning.

The east entrance to the Lyre Bridge, where Carpenter and Pokorny meet, is packed full of garbage, debris, rotten meat, and other assorted types of filth. A group of ragged beggars stand by, armed with torches.

Old Beggars. While several people are milling about at each location, only a few of these individuals are part of the Beggars Guild. There are **1d4 common beggars** and a **beggar journeyman** at each location. Add or subtract common beggars to make these encounters interesting for the players. The true guildsmen are on alert for city watch, vigilantes, and random adventurers. If provoked, the beggars fight back, initially with stink pots (see **Appendix B: New Items**) or debris to harass the attackers, but if pressed, they fight to kill. Any casualties are quickly dragged into the debris and covered so the watch doesn't immediately understand the escalation in hostilities.

Beggar Apprentices (Thf1) (1d4): HP 3; **AC** 7[12]; **Atk** dagger (1d4); **Move** 12; **Save** 15; **AL** N; **CL/XP** 1/15; **Special:** +2 save bonus vs. traps and magical devices, backstab (x2), thieving skills.

Thieving Skills: Climb 85%, Tasks/Traps 15%, Hear 3 in 6, Hide 10%, Silent 20%, Locks 10%.
Equipment: leather armor, dagger, 3 stink pots.
Beggar Journeyman (Thf3): HP 7; **HP** 40; **AC** 7[12]; **Atk** club (1d4) or dagger (1d4); **Move** 12; **Save** 13; **AL** N; **CL/XP** 3/60; **Special:** +2 save bonus vs. traps and magical devices, backstab (x2), thieving skills.
Thieving Skills: Climb 87%, Tasks/Traps 25%, Hear 4 in 6, Hide 20%, Silent 30%, Locks 20%.
Equipment: leather armor, club, dagger, 2 stink pots.

In the Interests of Beggars. The guild is attempting to gather attention from the surrounding districts that something is wrong in the Well. That beggars have gone missing with no official response is not unusual; what is unusual is the guild losing contact within their organization. These beggars are not just out of communication, they are gone.

This overt display of civic unrest is a sham. The guild wants the full might of the council to come down on the district; their true intent is to have the Wheelwrights driven from this side of the Stoneheart. Guildmaster Gromp is playing a long game and is willing to sacrifice some of his pawns to remove the other side's king.

The guild does not seek out the characters during this demonstration, despite their awareness of the party's investigation. If the party is affiliated with the Beggars or contacts a guildmember, the characters get an audience with Gromp.

Meeting Gromp. However the characters get to this point, they are granted an audience with **Lucius Gromp**, the Guildmaster of Beggars. The meeting happens in the guildhouse (**C13** in the Canal District), and characters must agree to hoods or blindfolds to enter. If they refuse, no meeting occurs.

Gromp is straightforward with his concerns; the Wheelwrights have an agent in the district, a rich individual with no known employment. This agent, Lassiter D'Torrance, is based in the "Gaunt House" (**Area TW41**) in Turlin's Well, and Gromp offers a runner who can show the characters to the house the following day when things calm down. Discrediting D'Torrance would go a long way toward ensuring that the Beggars get what they want. Gromp asks the characters to investigate the house, find some derogatory information — or plant some for the Watch to find — or in some other way bring a stain to the family name and drive the man from the city. He offers an exchange: The characters take care of D'Torrance, and they get to come to him three times for information. Their contract ends after this. He offers a crusted hand to "shake on it."

Guildmaster Lucius Gromp (Thf7): HP 20; AC 7[12]; **Atk** hand-hook (1d4); **Move** 12; **Save** 7; **AL** N; **CL/XP** 7/600; **Special:** +2 save bonus vs. traps and magical devices, backstab (x3), read languages, thieving skills.

Thieving Skills: Climb 91%, Tasks/Traps 45%, Hear 5 in 6, Hide 40%, Silent 50%, Locks 40%. **Equipment:** hand-hook (treat as dagger), *ring of protection +2*.

Clues. A Reliable Rumor. If the characters balk at Gromp's request, he suggests that there may be frequent comings and goings at the house, often on the nights of "great disturbance in the city," hinting that he knows even more than what he says. If pressed by the characters for additional aid, Gromp promises the characters that "I'll have eyes on you at all times."

DAY 9

SISTERSDAG, FREYRMOND 13

This is the day the characters enter the final act of this adventure. If the characters met with Gromp, the runner he promised meets the characters at wherever they are staying and leads them to Gaunt House. If they did not meet the guildmaster, use whatever setup is necessary to ensure that the characters find their way to their last major encounter in the city.

The Morning Of. The day begins quietly, a far cry from the previous day's insanity. A pall of smoke hangs in the air, and the sky is overcast. While dreary, there are no screams tearing through the streets. Normal city sounds greet the characters as they prep for their day. The party has the morning for any preparations they need to make. If the characters are staying at one of the district's inns, breakfast is waiting for them when they rise. If they are in other accommodations, something appropriate to the situation awaits them. If the characters ask about the repast, they are informed that "You have an admirer who arranged everything." No more information is left to be gathered. The food is safe and suits the establishment they are in. When the characters finish and are ready to investigate, proceed in getting them to Gaunt House.

GAUNT HOUSE — LAIR OF THE FIEND

*Gaunt House is **Area TW41** on the map.*

The last house along the northeastern row of canal houses, situated on the southern bank of the East Channel, Gaunt House's description lives up to its name. The structure is modeled in the Castorhagean aristocratic style. Weathered trim frames beige stucco walls and timeworn brick facades. Peaked roofs topped with archaic gargoyles loom above the two-story structure. The house has long been in decline, standing as a testament to fear of collapse. The place emanates *age*.

Gaunt House's main characteristic is its proximity to the Between, a terrifying border-reality that is described equally as Heaven or Hell, both or neither. While no gateways or mirror-portals exist in the house, the taint of the Between has leeched itself into the fibers of the structure. Terror and despair are atmospherically constant; the creepiness of the house goes beyond its physical disrepair and touches a primal part of any living being that enters. Additional information and flavor about the Between can be found in ***The Blight*** by **Frog God Games**.

Exploring Gaunt House opens the characters to a new threat: mental exhaustion. Mental exhaustion hampers a character and causes hallucinations, madness, or even catatonia. See the **Mental Exhaustion** sidebar for tracking the affliction. While intense and frightening effects are a staple of fantasy adventuring, the inclusion of the Between elevates these common terrors to an overwhelming level.

The Fiend of the House. The Fiend can be found anywhere in Gaunt House, or not here at all. Its knowledge of the layout and the side effects of the house are absolute; it can, and will, use Gaunt House to its advantage at any opportunity. The Fiend can be found anywhere, and unless badly harmed, it does not flee the grounds. It is a powerful foe for any party at this level. Only clever (and lucky!) characters stand a chance of driving it off and fighting another day.

***Between* Connection.** Because of the inundation of Between captured in Gaunt House, several odd, possibly dangerous effects can randomly occur. Roll 1d8 each time the characters enter a new room. On a roll of 1, have the first character entering the room roll 1d20 and consult the **A Little Bit Between** table:

A LITTLE BIT BETWEEN

1d20	Result
1.	A shadow falls the wrong way in the room.
2.	A puddle appears at your feet, momentarily reflecting a grinning face with wickedly sharp teeth. It instantly dries up.
3.	A fat, black fly lands close by, stares at you disturbingly, then slowly flies away.
4.	You're sure the doorknob said something rude.
5.	Somewhere in the city, a clock strikes fifteen. There are no clocks able to do that in Bard's Gate.
6.	Your shadow is momentarily monstrous but then returns to normal.
7.	Your hands begin to shake uncontrollable and feel intensely cold; then you suddenly return to normal.
8.	A horrific face forms under the wallpaper and then drifts away.
9.	You keep seeing something out of the corner of your eye — some sort of insect scuttling about the ceiling — but every time you look, it's gone.
10.	The smell of burning sugar is strong here.
11.	You're sure some *thing* called out your name, but there's no one else around.
12.	You're apparently the only one who hears the terrible scream.
13.	Your reflection in the polished wood is of something terrible; then when you glance again, it's back to normal.
14.	You keep hearing the same word in your ear every few minutes: "Soon."
15.	The same man in a top hat keeps waving to you from outside. If anyone investigates, he is gone, and there are no footprints.
16.	An enormous cobweb entirely covers a doorway.
17.	What is that strange flute music from the attic?
18.	You pass the third window in a row and see the same sobbing woman outside. She is not there if characters go outside and investigate.
19.	The buzzing continues in your head — sometimes louder, sometimes softer, but always menacing.
20.	The floor beneath your feet suddenly jolts, but no one else seems to notice.

MENTAL EXHAUSTION

A new condition introduced by Gaunt House's link to the Between is mental exhaustion. Mental exhaustion tracks how a character's mental state deteriorates through time, horrific events, physical trauma, or any sufficiently draining situation you devise. This condition has physical manifestations as well as mental, so the consequences can be quite severe.

Typically, a single event is not enough to inflict mental trauma; however, extremely ghastly events or overwhelming terror can begin the descent into madness. A traumatic event can give a creature one or more levels of mental exhaustion, as specified in the effect's description. Typically, a creature must make a saving throw to avoid the effect; failure adds or increases their current level of mental exhaustion as show in the table.

Level	Effect
1	Disadvantage on ability checks
2	Hallucinations
3	Disadvantage on attack rolls and saving throws
4	Madness
5	Insanity
6	Catatonia

If an already exhausted creature suffers another effect that causes mental exhaustion, its current level of exhaustion increases by the amount specified in the effect's description.

A creature suffers the effect of its current level of mental exhaustion as well as all lower levels. For example, a creature suffering Level 2 mental exhaustion begins hallucinating and has a −1 penalty on saving throws.

Mental exhaustion can be removed by resting, by removing oneself from the cause of the effects (such as by leaving Gaunt House), or by casting *remove curse* on the character.

Resting for one hour lowers a character's mental exhaustion level by 1, provided that the creature sleeps and that the traumatic event is not in continuous plain sight.

Hallucinations. The character sees and hears things that are not there. The hallucinations can be as vivid as your imagination; however, they should have some connection to the traumatic event. The hallucinations cannot harm the afflicted directly, although they may lead to dangerous situations.

Madness. The character loses a grasp on reality. Roll 1d8; on a roll of 1–3, the character suffers short-term madness; on a roll of 4–6, long-term madness; and a roll of 7–8 results in indefinite madness. The effects of the character's madness are left up to you to determine.

Insanity. The afflicted is insane. An insane creature can't take actions, can't understand what other creatures say, can't read, and speaks only in gibberish. You control its movement, which is erratic and unpredictable.

Catatonia. The mental exhaustion is too much. The character's mind retreats deep within itself and the body loses function. The character slips into a coma-like state until they receive magical healing. *Restoration, limited wish,* or similar magic cures the affliction.

TW41-1. ENTRY

A beautifully carved hardwood door provides entry into the house. The door is swollen from moisture and disuse, so a combined 21 strength is required to open it. The door is not locked, trapped, or dangerous. The front door has not been used in some time. It creaks loudly upon opening, in addition to any noise made while forcing it open.

TW41-2. FOYER

If the characters break through the front door, they enter a charming, antiquated foyer. A threadbare carpet runner leads from the door to the gallery, covering creaking hardwood flooring. The flooring gives disadvantage on all Stealth checks in this area. The ceiling is open to the looming, second-floor balcony. The air is thick with dust and tastes slightly of dried flowers. The smell of dust is prevalent. Sparse cobwebs decorate the walls and corners of the room.

The Floor Tells a Tale. If the runner is moved, characters notice a stained outline on the hardwood. The outline is in a vaguely humanoid shape, but oddly proportioned. This is likely a large bloodstain. One of the Fiend's victims was killed here and left to bleed out.

Mental Exhaustion. Discovering the stain of the Fiend's victim wouldn't normally be so traumatic, but proximity to the Between makes the discovery more vibrant. The character initially discovering the stain is nearly overwhelmed with visions of the victim's last moments. Sensations of terror, the smell of blood, dust, and decay fill the character's mind with horrifying images. They *feel* as if *they* are on the floor looking up at a shadowy man stalking forward, a huge hammer in his hand. When the image focuses, the character sees that the hammer *is* the killer's hand.

The character (or characters if several investigate the floor) must make a saving throw. If successful, the visions clear, and reality slowly creeps back in. If the save fails, the images take hold, the Between infects the character's mind, and they suffer 1 level of mental exhaustion.

Stairs to the Upper Gallery. A winding staircase ascends to another gallery on the second floor. The stairs are creaky but stable; they groan loudly when walked upon. The stairs are covered in thin, stained carpeting.

TW41-3. GREETING ROOM

This is a comfortable, outdated, and dusty drawing room off the foyer. Overstuffed chairs and a couch are arranged around the perimeter, covered in what was once white linen, now dust encrusted and yellowed with age. Grimy windows look out to the east, flanked with thick, dark drapes. Various pictures adorn the wood-panel walls, and assorted bric-a-brac litters small tables around the room. A pocket door in the west wall is the only exit from the room. There is a heavy, foreboding feeling here. It smells stale, as if no one has been in the room for an age.

Treasure. The assorted knickknacks are worth a total of 4d8 gp.

TW41-4. MESSAGE HALL

The house staff used this short hallway to pass messages to guests waiting in the drawing room.

Sliding Doors. Pocket doors in the east and west walls of the hallway move smoothly on hidden runners in the ceiling. The doors are well-oiled and appear almost new. The doors are oddly affected by the Between; the wood does not degrade like the surrounding house.

TW41-5. CLOSET (BETWEEN WAYPOINT)

At first glance, this appears to be a standard cloakroom.

If characters enter the closet, they experience a subtle feeling of chill and vertigo at the same time. They have entered a space-between-spaces; they are in a Between waypoint.

Waypoint. This area has a bizarre effect courtesy of the Between. Characters entering the closet and closing the door discover that they can travel to another part of Gaunt House. Once the door is closed, the character can concentrate on another of the waypoints (**Areas TW41-10A** or **TW41-19A**), open the door, and step out in the new location. The effect is similar to a *teleport* spell, except there is no chance of a mishap. Traveling this way has a cost: When a character switches locations, the Between notices. Characters need to make a successful saving throw or suffer 1 level of mental exhaustion.

Initially, the characters will have no knowledge of how to travel through the house using this method. Without an experienced traveler, a character can roll below his or her intelligence on 4d6. A success gives the character a mental glimpse of the other waypoints, and if they concentrate on a location, they feel a slight pulling sensation and arrive in the new point. Failure indicates no movement, and the character may exit the closet normally, possibly assuming the closet is just an "odd space" in the house.

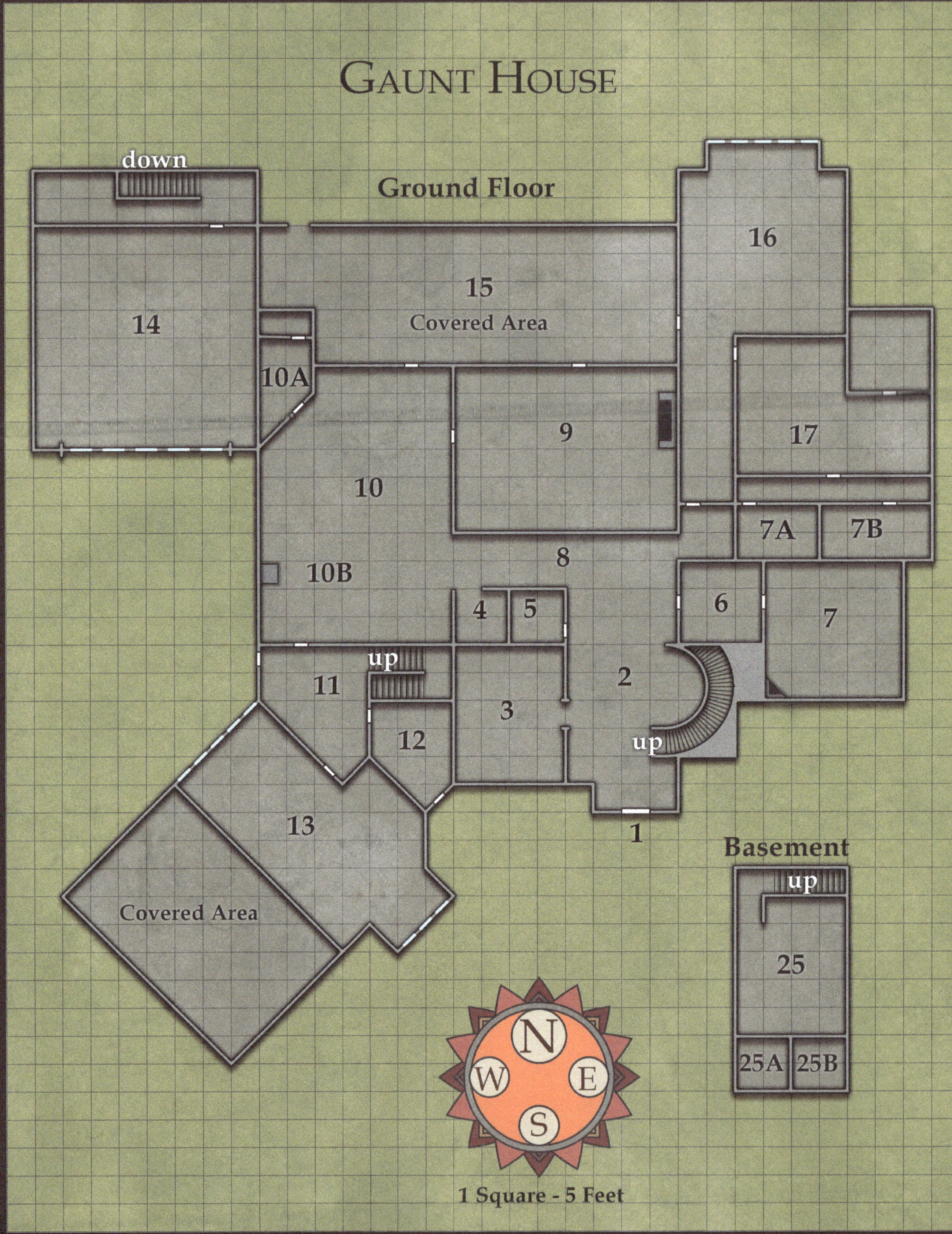

Gaunt House
down
Ground Floor
16
15
Covered Area
14
10A
17
9
10
7A
7B
8
6
10B
7
4
5
2
up
11
3
up
12
1
13
Basement
up
Covered Area
25
N
W
E
S
25A
25B
1 Square - 5 Feet

TW41-6. Vestibule

This passage leads from the foyer into the study. An open closet is in the east wall. Whimpering can be heard from inside when the characters approach.

Unexpected Visitor. A huddled figure is facing the back corner of the closet, cloaks and robes piled upon it. It does not move initially, but if characters remove the clothes for a better look, the **ghoul** turns and attacks. The ghoul is covered in scars and old wounds, and protruding bones augment the horrific nature of the undead.

This ragged creature is one of the forgotten beggars that has been missing for several weeks. He was abducted long before the start of the vandalism and is unidentifiable in his current state. Strangely enough, it has no eyes. If somehow returned to the Beggars Guild, the characters are given a token thanks, and the body is disposed of.

Ghoul: HD 2; HP 13; AC 6[13]; Atk 2 claws (1d3 + paralysis), bite (1d4); **Move** 9; **Save** 16; **AL** C; **CL/XP** 3/60; **Special:** immunities (charm and sleep), paralyzing touch (3d6 turns, save avoids). (*Monstrosities* 191)

Treasure. A few of the cloaks are fur-lined, of decent quality, and not terribly stained; three of the cloaks are worth 25 gp each.

TW41-7. Study

This cozy chamber has a cold and unused fireplace in one corner. Fine leather chairs and several tables are spread through the room. A formal suit of plate armor stands in the northwest corner behind a luxurious couch. A broken window allows some air to flow into the room. A thick-piled carpet festooned with fleas and mites is laid out before the fireplace.

Obvious Guardian. The **animated armor** in the corner likely draws the party's attention. The armor animates when characters enter the room, requiring one round to move the couch before it can engage. The armor does not follow characters out of the room. It resets any moved furniture if all living beings leave the room.

Animated Armor: HD 4; HP 27; AC 5[14]; **Atk** longsword (1d8); **Move** 6; **Save** 16; **AL** N; **CL/XP** 4/120; **Special:** none.

Fireplace. The chimney has a narrow flue that provides access to the roof. A halfling or dwarf can ascend at 50% their normal movement rate. Smaller creatures can move at 75% normal.

TW41-8. Gallery

This hallway links the larger rooms of Gaunt House. Pictures hang on the walls in a chaotic jumble of images, overwhelming in their disparity. Some of the pictures are from famous artists and quite valuable, while others are simple sketches and worthless. There does not appear to be a coherent theme of the display; it's a riot of color, shapes, landscapes, and less-understood images.

Storyboard. The art in the gallery largely makes no sense to onlookers. However, any character suffering from at least 1 level of mental exhaustion sees truth in the madness. Some of the sketches seem to depict scenes currently plaguing the Well; for example, a small portrait shows the scene of the gruesome package from a bird's-eye perspective. If the characters participated in that encounter, they are shown as onlookers in the crowd. A color impressionist landscape shows Turlin's Well at dusk, clearly capturing the party out walking or patrolling. A large, black-and-white scene shows a vista overlooking the island around Castorhage, a small ship approaching from the direction of Reme. The ship, if studied carefully, is revealed to be *The Flight of Oberon*.

If none of the characters is suffering from mental exhaustion, the gallery appears as a well-rendered mess that lacks any consistent design theme.

Mental Exhaustion. Onlookers have a 30% chance to notice their own likenesses in the art. The paintings featuring the characters are not new, so the revelation that actions they just undertook are captured in paint is overwhelming. Characters who notice their images must make a saving throw. If successful, they are able to shudder off the thoughts that they have been following a pre-determined script; if unsuccessful, they suffer 1 level of mental exhaustion.

Treasure. There are 1d6 paintings that, despite their disturbing nature, are professionally rendered. If gathered and sold to an art dealer in town (who doesn't know where they came from), they can be sold for 1d4+1 x 100 gp each. The other 20 pieces are worth 1d4 x 10 gp each.

TW41-9. Chapel

This is a sunken area, with three steps leading down to a floor covered in sigils, runes, and glyphs. The walls are adorned with additional runes, shapes, and vividly obscene images. A heavy miasma of decay, blood, and something less definable lingers in the air. A large fireplace is in the north wall, with heavy chains anchored to the stone mantel. Black iron sconces protrude from the corners of the room. An iron chandelier hangs from a stout chain in the ceiling. A passage opens to the south, and a door is in the west wall. The room is warmer than other areas, although the fireplace has not seen recent use.

The Engraved Floor. If the characters proceed into the room, additional details about the floor are visible. A fine silver vein runs along the edge of the floor where it meets the bottom step. A character investigating the silver vein and the sigils and runes painted on the floor understands that the whole is designed to be a large summoning or magical containment area. Disturbingly, the runes and sigils are drawn with the intent to keep something *in*, not *out*.

Further investigation reveals eight rectangular shapes engraved in the stone floor. If characters break through the floor, they expose entombed corpses. The corpses are desiccated, and the cause of death was blunt trauma to the head. The bodies have been here for many years; the ceremonial shrouds wrapping the victims are withered and putrefied.

Woken Dead. If the characters physically disturb any of the bodies, the corpses all shudder and attempt to rise out of their tombs. Characters have one round of free attacks on the **8 cadavers** before they free themselves from the shallow graves and attack. If the characters defeat the cadavers but do not use magic weapons or spells, the bodies lie inert in their tombs until they regain their full hit points, then set out after the characters if they remain in the house. They do not pursue characters outside of Gaunt House.

Cadaver (8): HD 2; HP 14, 12x2, 10, 9, 7x3; AC 6[13]; **Atk** 2 claws (1d4 + disease), bite (1d6 + disease); **Move** 6; **Save** 16; **AL** C; **CL/XP** 4/120; **Special:** disease (wasting, 1d4 damage, save resists), reincarnation (regain 1hp per round until restored). (see **Appendix A: New Monster**)

Gothic Lighting Reveals. The sconces and chandelier are crafted in an unusual artistic style. Details suggest architecture commonly depicted in texts describing the Hells, which mention that several ornate talismans exist to capture devils, binding them to their captor's will. The metal is bent into shapes in a style well-documented in Infernal literature. The iron in these items is not from this plane of existence.

Mental Exhaustion. Few locations in the city limits are as disturbing as this room. As the characters uncover more of the liturgy here, the more they open themselves to its malign influence. Upon observing the mass of glyphs and sigils covering the room, characters begin to feel a creeping dread, a sense of claustrophobia — as if the house is narrowing, closing in on them. Creaks and groans become more pronounced, the smell of *old* becomes thick in the air, and a deep weariness creeps into the characters' bones. Characters failing a saving throws gain 1 level of mental exhaustion. Any character making a successful save still feels the emotional drain but suffers no other effects.

Characters witnessing the dead rise from their crypts must make a saving throw. Successful saves embolden the characters; they are heroes after all! Failure indicates that the characters make future mental exhaustion checks with a –1 penalty until they take a long rest.

Treasure. If removed, the sconces and chandelier are worth 2,500 gp for their craftsmanship. However, these items are exceedingly tainted with evil, and good-aligned characters should have a problem selling them. If broken up for their component metal, the objects are worth 150 gp in raw material cost. The four sconces weigh two pounds each, and the chandelier weighs 250 pounds.

TW41-10. DINING ROOM

This is a large formal dining room. Dozens of chairs surround a table that is five feet wide and 10 feet long. Three table settings are placed on a yellowed tablecloth, although two are covered in dust. The walls are unadorned but covered in a slightly greasy filth. There is a door to the southwest, another in the west wall, and the eastern half of the room is a sparse kitchen. A grimy window is in the southern wall near the kitchen. A faint smell of cooked meat lingers in the air; under these circumstances, it is *not* a pleasant odor.

Dining Table. The dishes are valuable, if rather gaudy. The flatware is simple metal of no value. The glassware is an old, aristocratic style long out of vogue. The table covering is yellowed with age and neglect, but is sturdy cloth that has maintained its integrity. The table itself is a sturdy, plain slab construction popular in the late 3300s in Castorhage.

Under the table — and gaining surprise if no one suggests prodding the hanging tablecloth — is a **giant spider**. It attacks once, and then tries to escape by crawling to the ceiling. The spider moves in a jittering, spastic way, as if it's not in control of its own body.

Giant Spider (4ft diameter): HD 2+2; **HP** 14; **AC** 6[13]; **Atk** bite (1d6 + poison); **Move** 18; **Save** 16; **AL** N; **CL/XP** 5/240; **Special:** lethal poison (save or die, +1 saving throw), surprise prey (5-in-6 chance). (*Monstrosities* 451)

Treasure. The table settings are worth 500 gp to a collector due to their vintage.

TW41-10A. PANTRY (BETWEEN WAYPOINT)

Upon entering this area off the dining room, characters notice shelves of dry goods, moldy cheese, stale and petrified breads, and other inedible fare. If all three doors are closed at the same time, the truth of the room becomes apparent.

Waypoint. This area has a bizarre effect courtesy of the Between. Characters entering the pantry and closing the doors discover that they can travel to another part of Gaunt House. Once the doors are closed, the character can concentrate on another of the waypoints (**Areas TW41-5** or **TW41-19A**), open the door, and step out in the new location. The effect is similar to a *teleport* spell, except there is no chance of a mishap. Traveling in this way has a cost; when a character switches locations, the Between notices. Characters need to make a successful saving throw or suffer 1 level of mental exhaustion.

See **Area TW41-5** if this is the first time the characters attempt to use a waypoint.

Exit. The door in the south wall leads to the sunroom. It has a sturdy bolt on this side.

TW41-10B. KITCHEN

This area is a simple kitchen. A low counter runs along the east and north walls. The south wall holds a cabinet intended to store ice. A central island dominates the workspace. A pocket door leads out through the east wall, and a doorway leads to the gallery (**Area TW41-8**).

Counter Intuitive. If the characters investigate the counter area, they discover that a large amount of butchering has been performed recently. A few cooking utensils are strewn about the counter, and they discover the presence of several medical tools as well.

The ice cabinet is very cool if approached. Opening the cabinet exposes several large blocks of ice, some smaller chips of ice, and 13 paper-wrapped packages. Each two-pound paper bundle contains sections of freshly butchered meat. It is not immediately apparent from what kind of animal this meat is taken.

The Island. A countertop in the central island surrounds a small firepit. Several metal skewers surround the cooking area. Bits of meat — or some other flesh — have recently been cooked on them. Cabinets make up the bottom of the island, and they contain various pots, pans, plates, cooking utensils, and carving knives. All the cooking tools are stained and encrusted with unknown "foodstuff."

Cooking Staff? If characters search the cabinets, the second door opened releases a **swarm of rats**. The nearly starved animals present little threat to the characters; however, the rats carry sewer plague, which requires a saving throw after a bite to avoid an infection that causes 1d4 points of damage each day until healed.

Swarm of Rats: HD 5; **HP** 31; **AC** 7[12]; **Atk** bite (2d6 + disease); **Move** 9; **Save** 12; **AL** N; **CL/XP** 5/240; **Special:** disease (save or take 1d4 points of damage per day until healed).

Dumbwaiter. A small elevator is in the southeast corner of the kitchen. This dumbwaiter-contraption allows access to the second floor, outside the guest room closet (**Area TW41-21A**).

Treasure. All the cooking utensils, cutlery, pots and pans, and other accoutrements can be sold to an inn or restaurant for 250 gp once they are cleaned.

TW41-11. LANDING AND STAIRS

This antechamber is a landing for the stairs leading up to the second floor. A small, halfling-sized door is underneath the stairs. A padlock and hasp secure the portal. Another door in the south wall leads outside. A closet is in the northeast corner.

The Door Under the Stairs. The small door is closed with a padlock and requires a delicate, small key. The lock is trapped, with a thin slot in the side. If the trap is triggered, a small blade pops out of the side of the lock to slash at any creature holding it. The slashing blade does 1 point of damage and leaves the character unable to use the injured hand until they bandage it properly.

The Figure Under the Stairs. The small door creaks when it opens to expose a lightless, dusty space. Propped in the northwest corner of the cramped space is a tiny figure: a twig and string toy twisted into a bipedal shape and wrapped with bits of cloth.

Characters who roll below their wisdom on 3d6 realize the cloth looks familiar and notice that it is from another character's cloak or clothing (determine at random or choose one character).

Mental Exhaustion. Finding a tiny stick-doll wearing a piece of the character's own clothes in a locked room under some stairs requires that character to make a successful saving throw or suffer 1 level of mental exhaustion.

Treasure. The padlock is of high quality and worth 50 gp.

TW41-12. CLOSET

This is a large cloakroom. Various boots are tossed about, and cloaks, robes, and other outerwear are hung on pegs along the walls. Assorted wide-brim hats are on stands in the corners.

Dirty Laundry. Several bloody articles of clothing are barely hidden under a pile of boots in the easternmost corner. The blood is still damp, but the edges are dry. The blood is four to five days old. It is from the wererat victim in the assault.

TW41-13. WORKROOM

The first thing characters notice when they enter this room is the stark-white tiles covering all surfaces except the ceiling. A large bay window is in the southwest wall and looks out toward the sunroom. Another large window in the northeast wall faces the entry. A door in the same wall leads out to the front of the house, and another door in the southeast wall leads outside to a covered patio area. Several wheeled metal tables are against the southeast wall. The floor slopes slightly to the center of the room to an iron grate. Various shelves and hanging hooks line the northwest wall.

Worktables. The metal tables are study devices. They can each easily support 500 pounds. The wheels are well-maintained, and the tables are easily maneuvered, even when carrying heavy weights. The wheels are small, so rough terrain could pose a problem.

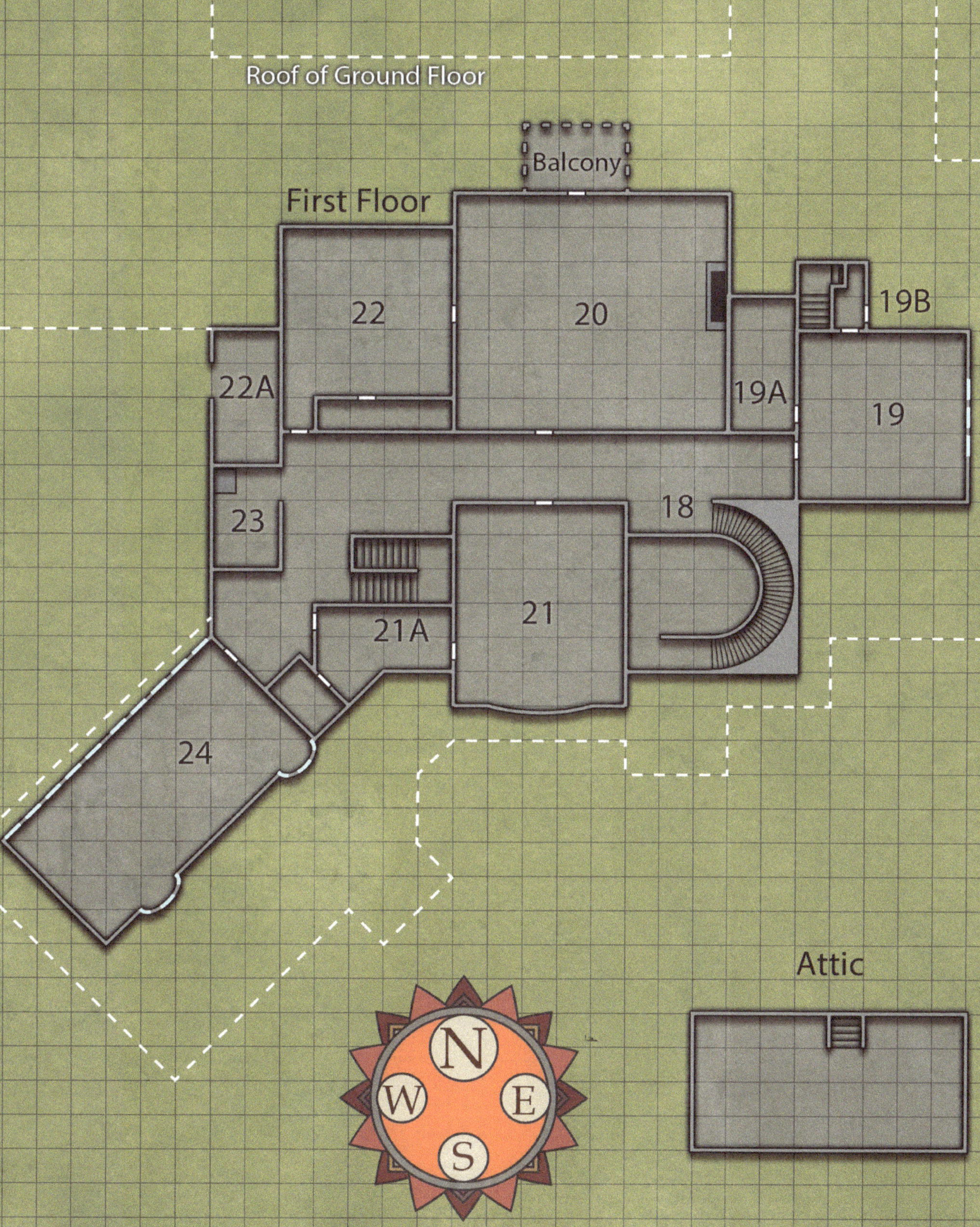
GAUNT HOUSE
Roof of Ground Floor
First Floor
Balcony
22
20
19B
22A
19A
19
23
18
21A
21
24
N
W
E
S
Attic
1 Square - 5 Feet

Tools of the Trade. All the tools and devices in this room are useful for butchering and moving livestock. The entire room is easily washed down to the main drain in the center of the floor. Several of the tools are stained from excessive use. A broken bottle on one of the shelves contains the residue of the paralytic poison used on the wererat (see **The Assault**).

Treasure. The tools and tables could be sold for 200 gp.

TW41-14. Sunroom

This area of large windows is a sunroom or solarium. Thick rugs cover most of the floor space, while wicker-and-reed furniture adorns the room's perimeter. The center of the room features a cushioned settee. A partially

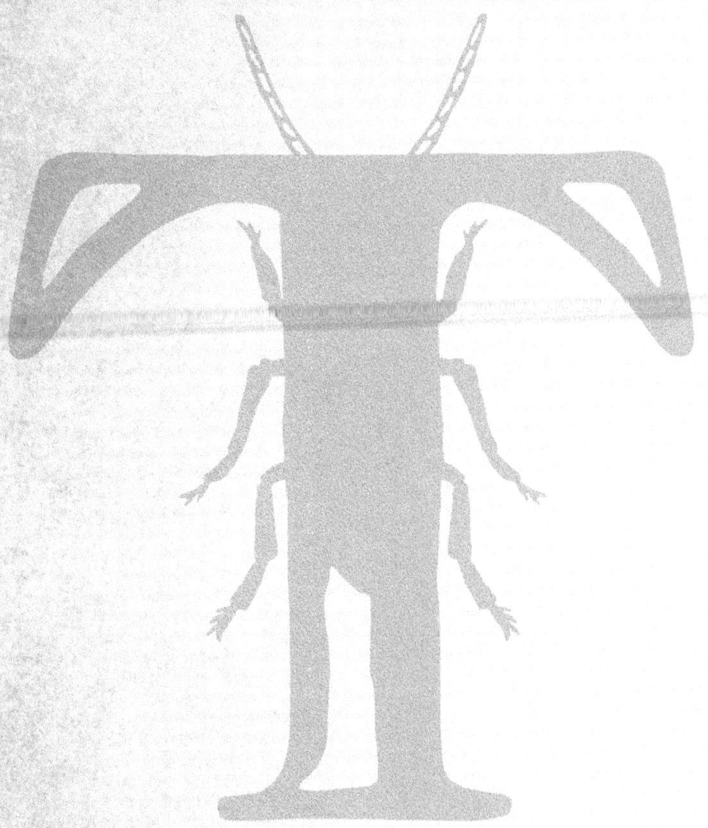

completed sketch sits on an easel off to one side. A stout wooden door with several locks plainly visible is in the west wall.

The Sketch. The sketch depicts a detailed landscape of the Castorhage skyline. Several buildings are shown in detail, with an indistinct smudge effect distorting the whole. The sketch is good, but not master-quality. There are six additional sheets of drawing paper and a dozen pieces of charcoal of various hardness.

The Door. The wooden door is obviously of quality construction and seems stout. The slab itself is plain, but intricate script is engraved in the jam surrounding the door. The hinges of the door are on this side. The door opens into this room; it is designed to keep something from getting in here from wherever it leads. The three locks and two bolts are easily opened from this side.

If the door is opened, it reveals a small landing and stairs leading down into darkness. The steps are made of wood, and a gut-twisting, putrid odor rises from below. The air is slightly damp and stagnant. Ambient light from the sunroom barely illuminates the stairwell.

The Floor. The floor under the rugs is exotic hardwood from the north. It is highly polished and in remarkable condition. Underneath the rugs, the floor is engraved with many runes and glyphs. The runes are typical of druids and ancient, primal deities. The runes and glyphs are intended to appease dark fairy folk. While this is not enough to require a mental exhaustion check, it does give characters a very uneasy feeling.

Treasure. The sketching papers are excellent quality and worth 5 gp per sheet. The charcoal is quite useful and worth 10 gp in total. The easel and furniture are worth 25 gp. The sketch itself, if sold, fetches 10 gp.

TW41-15. Covered Veranda

An open exterior area, this veranda is protected from the weather and from observation. A large fireplace is in the north wall, and a small, open storage area is in the south wall. A few short steps lead down to the surrounding grounds.

Fireplace. The firebox is sooty and shows signs of recent use. Some unburned scraps of cloth can be discovered that look as if they could be from clothing.

TW41-16. Master Bedroom

This room is the main area of the "master suite." A large bed piled high with pillows and blankets dominates a spacious sleeping area. An armoire and a closet sit along the south wall. Windows fill the west wall, with two additional windows looking north. A door leads outside to the veranda, and passages to the gallery and the privy head off in the east wall. An unpleasant smell emanates from the bed area. The north wall features a landscape painting of Castorhage, with a dusky, evening tone.

The Bed. If characters approach the bed to investigate the terrible stench, they learn it is the smell is of excrement. Further investigation of the bed and removing the piles of blankets and skins covering the top reveals that it is not a bed; the blankets are covering a two-foot-tall cage that is six feet long and six feet wide. Two prisoners — a male and a female human — are in the cage. An overflowing bucket of waste is in one corner.

Prisoners. The man and woman are unresponsive to questioning. They barely register the characters' presence and are not communicative in any way. Each is suffering from 5 levels of mental exhaustion; they are not quite comatose, but the constant sensory overload of being held captive in the tiny cage keeps them from recovering. They are **commoners** and currently have 1 hp each.

If the prisoners are healed enough to allow them to be questioned, they weave quite a tale. Both are beggars, low-level guildmembers who were in the wrong place at the wrong time. They were drugged and captured, and later awoke in a dark tiny cell (the cage under the bed). They have no idea how much time has passed since they were captured but they can eventually determine that they have been prisoners for almost two full weeks.

Commoners, Human Male and Female Beggars: HP 4, 3 (currently 1 each); **AC** 9[10]; **Atk** weapon (1d6); **Move** 12; **Save** 18; **AL** Any; **CL/XP** B/10; **Special:** none. (**Monstrosities** 254)

Bedroom Furniture. The furniture is large and sturdy but plain. The closet holds a few nightshirts and robes while the armoire is full of aristocratic-styled dress. The clothes are moth-eaten and dingy, but serviceable.

Mental Exhaustion. Discovering the prisoners' condition and understanding the depths of sadism required to confine them in such a manner requires all the characters to make a successful saving throw or suffer 1 level of mental exhaustion.

Treasure. The large Castorhagean landscape is worth 1,500 gp. The armoire and closet could be sold to an inn for 150 gp each. They weigh 200 pounds each.

TW41-17. Master Closet

Various articles of clothing are stored here. Robes, cloaks, several full outfits for men and women, and a plethora of shoes and boots are all arranged in this large closet. A small alcove in the northwest wall is a "jewelry room" with several pieces of ornate, if gaudy, necklaces, bracelets, tiaras, and other audacious pieces.

Treasure. The jewelry is costume paste-and-glass fabrications. The clothes and jewelry could be sold in Bard's Gate to a playhouse as costumes for 250 gp.

TW41-17A. Men's Privy

This is a "men's room." It is very clean and looks unused for some time. There is a small table with a pitcher of stale water and washbasin. There are no towels to dry hands.

TW41-17B. Lady's Privy

This is a "ladies' room." It is very clean but smells as if it has been used recently. There is a small table with a pitcher of stale water and washbasin. There are no towels to dry hands.

Lavatory Table. The lavatory table is secretly a **mimic**. The creature is what is exuding the excrement smell. It has been crawling out of the privy to devour the excess waste from the prisoners in the master bedroom. The mimic attacks any characters who open the door and investigate the room. The creature does not leave the room to initiate attacks, but it does follow characters out of the room if engaged in combat.

Mimic: HD 7; HP 43; AC 6[13]; **Atk** smash (2d6); **Move** 2; **Save** 9; **AL** N; **CL/XP** 8/800; **Special:** glue (save or stuck to mimic), mimicry (disguise as various items). (*Monstrosities* 329)

TW41-18. Upper Gallery

Similar to the gallery on the first floor, this hallway is a haphazard arrangement of visual images of varying quality. A uniform theme of the diabolic is notable, with several landscapes depicting "classical" representations of various demon princes.

The Signature. The signature on the paintings is actually the sigil of the Demon-Princess Teratashia, who is not one of the great demons included in any of the pictures.

Treasure. Much like the lower gallery, the paintings, while distasteful and disturbing, are of professional quality. If sold to an art dealer (who doesn't know where they came from), 2d6 paintings can be sold for 2d4+1 x 100 gp each. The other 10 pieces are worth 2d4 x 10 gp each.

TW41-19. Guest Room

This guest room is comfortable looking, if a bit spartan. A single narrow bed is against the east wall, with doors in the south and west walls. A window in the north wall is covered by parchment to filter incoming light. An unpleasant odor emanates from behind the western door.

TW41-19A. Closet (Between Waypoint)

This is a standard closet with cloaks and boots in perfect order. The room doubles as a small privy for guests.

Waypoint. This area has a bizarre effect courtesy of the Between. Characters entering the closet and closing the door discover they can travel to another part of Gaunt House. Once the door is closed, the character can concentrate on another of the waypoints (**Areas TW41-5** or **TW41-10A**), open the door, and step out in the new location. The effect is similar to a *teleport* spell, except there is no chance of a mishap. Traveling this way has a cost; when a character switches locations, the Between notices. Characters need to make a successful saving throw or suffer 1 level of mental exhaustion.

See **Area TW41-5** if this is the first time characters attempt to use a waypoint.

TW41-19B. Attic Access

A small door in the west wall of the guest room leads into Gaunt House's attic space.

The Small Door. Characters who listen at the door gain two bits of information. The first is a slight buzzing sound from the other side of the door. The other is an increase in the awful odor noticeable in the room.

If the unlocked door is opened, a horrible stench erupts from the attic space, along with a swarm of flies. The insects do no harm but are disorienting and irritating. The flies stay in the guest room unless the window is opened or if the door to the upper gallery is left open.

TW41-19C. Attic

The ceiling of the attic space is four feet tall, which requires characters to stoop if they enter the space. Numerous boxes and crates are stored in the attic, as well as pieces of furniture covered with aging and tattered cloth. Characters must squeeze to move through the attic space. Small characters can move through the area with no impediments.

The stench intensifies in the far western portion of the attic. A flickering light can be seen over and around the items stored up here. If the party approaches, they discover a liturgy of glyphs and sigils arranged on the floor, the west wall, and the ceiling. Four lit black candles are burning at the cardinal points. A chalice of blood is placed next to one candle. A humanoid figure is lying on the sigils on the floor.

The Sacrifice. Investigating the figure reveals that it is a human male approximately 50 years of age. He is breathing shallowly and erratically. There is a slight discoloration around the victim's mouth. A large incision in the chest is held closed by amateurish, oversized stitches.

Characters investigating either of these conditions discovers the discoloration is likely the same as the wererat involved in the **Gruesome Package** encounter. The discoloration is from a paralytic poison. The incision and the accompanying stitches are meaningless; the victim was cut open only for show, and there is no internal injury. The stitches are designed to confuse any rescuers and to terrify the victim.

The victim's name is **Ectarr D'Miean**, a lesser nephew of the D'Miean family of Castorhage. He is a low-level merchant and importer, and a deplorable human being guilty of low morality. No excess is beyond this cretin. If rescued, he offers the characters a 500 gp reward.

Ectarr D'Miean, Human Male Noble: HP 29 (currently 1); AC 9[10]; **Atk** weapon (1d6); **Move** 12; **Save** 12; **AL** N; **CL/XP** 5/240; **Special:** none. (*Monstrosities* 254)

Mental Exhaustion. Discovering the false ritualistic sacrifice, staged perfectly for maximum effect, requires all characters witnessing the scene to make a saving throw or suffer 1 level of mental exhaustion.

TW41-20. Lounge

Double doors lead into this large room, which has a massive, ornate fireplace along the north wall. Fashioned of iron and stone, the chimney is formed to represent a demon; it is a statue of Teratashia. The demon-princess has the body of a cockroach and the head of a human female, although the features are twisted and distorted. A necklace of skulls hangs around the neck of the statue, and they look real.

A door leads outside to a balcony overlooking the lower veranda. A wrought-iron handrail surrounds the deck, which offers an excellent panoramic view of the Outer District. Several divans and chairs are situated around the perimeter of the room, and garish and highly suggestive paintings hang around the walls.

Treasure. The six paintings, while disturbing, are very well rendered. They are master-level quality and are worth 2,000 gp each.

TW41-21. Guest Room

This guest room is luxuriously appointed. Pillows and cushions are piled high on the grand bed along the north wall. Thick, well-cushioned carpet fills the room from wall to wall. A short bench is along the south wall with several sets of plush slippers at the foot. A large bay window in the east wall is clear and clean, allowing the bright daylight to illuminate the room. A pocket door is in the south wall, and a large mirror takes up most of the west wall not occupied by the entry door. The room is clean and appears to be well-maintained. It does not look to have seen recent use.

The Bed. The bed is covered in pillows, cushions, pads, and other sleep accessories. A rich fur comforter is below the mounded pillows. If the bed is investigated, removing the pillows betrays its hidden secret: the disfigured corpse of a human male is under the pile of cushions.

The Victim. This was Emil Orimus, a member of the Beggars Guild who got too close to the Fiend. Emil found it odd that a lone traveler was unafraid of walking through the Well at night and followed him to Gaunt House. After suffering through the traumas inflicted by the house, Emil was in a vastly weakened state when the Fiend began practicing its new hobby of vivisection.

Emil is a mess. Internal organs are exposed, bones are sawed-through, broken-off, and splayed about. Flesh is peeled and twisted, the whole appearing to be some form of atrocious medical experimentation. Fortunately, Emil perished at some point in the process.

The Vengeance. Emil may no longer be alive, but he's not finished yet. Emil transformed into a **wight** and attacks the characters when they discover him. He attacks until all the characters are dead. If encountered during the day, Emil make all attacks in this room at disadvantage due to the window allowing so much light into the room.

Emil Orimus, Wight: HD 3; HP 15; AC 5[14]; **Atk** claw (1hp + level drain); **Move** 9; **Save** 14; **AL** C; **CL/XP** 6/400; **Special:** +1 or better magic or silver weapons to hit, level drain (1 level with hit). (*Monstrosities* 510)

Treasure. The covers and sheets — accessible if all the pillows are removed — are fine cloth, smooth and elegant. If cleaned, they can be sold for 200 gp.

TW41-21A. Closet/Passage

This area is a passthrough closet. A pocket door leading from the guest room (**Area TW41-21**) enters a narrow closet area. Another door farther south leads out to the landing area outside the lair of the Fiend (**Area TW41-24**). The balcony and the top of the stairs are to the west of the door.

Treasure. Various complete sets of aristocratic outfits can be gathered in the closet. The total value of all the items is 400 gp.

TW41-22. Guest Room

This area appears to be another main guest room. As soon as characters open the door, they are overwhelmed with the putrescence. This room is wall-to-wall filth and refuse. Garbage, carrion, and other less-identifiable masses are piled all over the room. Bits of broken furniture protrude from heaving mounds of egesta. Offal, excrement, and other fluids run down the walls and pool on the floor. If the characters enter the room, the disgusting mass spasmodically shifts, causing the room to undulate and groan. It is as if the room is an active ulcer in Gaunt House.

Windows to the Soul. The large bank of windows in the west wall is an enigma. Random flashes of scenes appear in the windows. The flashes cannot be of this reality; monsters, landscapes, and hideous images flash and pulse in an oddly erratic manner.

If characters wait and watch the scenes for longer than a minute, the profound sensory overload lessens. A single vague image of an iron gate clarifies, drawing viewers closer. It remains indistinct, just slightly out of focus, and then suddenly is crystal clear.

Mental Exhaustion. The immediate purity of the vision is overwhelming; characters monitoring the window must make a successful saving throw or suffer 1 level of mental exhaustion.

TW41-22A. Secret Closet

A well-concealed door is camouflaged in the filth and ordure covering the walls. A pocket door is in the south wall. The small area beyond is a stark contrast to the putrescence in the preceding room. This area is clean and stark, an orderly dressing area containing decent clothes, costumes, and a few random toys. The closet seems like it would be appropriate for an aristocratic child's room, leaving some concern for what is wrong with the previous room.

TW41-23. Kitchen Closet

This closet area houses a dumbwaiter that provides simple access to the kitchen (**Area TW41-10B**). A small character under 50 pounds could use the dumbwaiter to access both areas. The device needs service; its operation is jerky and noisy.

TW41-24. Lair of The Fiend

This large room off the southeast corner of Gaunt House is the main lair of the Fiend. A thick oak door opens into a well-lit, long, narrow room. Several floor-to-ceiling windows ring the perimeter, with smaller, dormer-style windows higher in the ceiling. No other doors are immediately visible. The floor is dark hardwood, with intricate wainscoting along the walls. The room gives off a relaxing "lounge" feel. Several overstuffed chairs are available, with a single long couch along the southwest wall. A small, elegant bar cabinet sits in the southeast corner. What looks like a birdcage hangs in the southwest corner. It is covered by a thick, dark blanket, and a quiet chittering can be heard from underneath.

The Birdcage. A large, covered birdcage in a corner of the main room hangs by a chain from a ceiling beam. The thick blanket covering the cage is dusty; it has not been removed in some time. If characters approach, they notice that the chittering occurs in a pattern that somewhat resembles a speaking cadence. A ranger or elf character realizes that the chittering sound is not from any normal avian.

One in Hand. If the characters remove the heavy cover, they see a small bat hanging upside down in the cage. Its feet grip the top of the cage, and it seems to be engaging in conversation with the characters. Anyone able to *speak with animals* or possessing some way to communicate with the bat immediately understands that the creature is muttering to itself. It is carrying on a lengthy diatribe about "The foolishness of getting caught" and "How can I escape?" and similar thoughts.

The "bat" is actually a polymorphed **quasit** named Dun Rathmon. The quasit was originally the familiar of Lassiter D'Torrance, although (being a demon) he bears Torad Yarog no ill will for killing its one-time master. He tries to lure the characters into pursuing the Fiend, without caring whether they kill the Fiend and avenge Lassiter or whether the Fiend kills them and he can take credit for bringing them. Either way, the quasit manages to spread chaos.

If the characters communicate with the quasit in his animal form, he quickly changes shape into a small humanoid. Dun tries to speak with the characters, but tries only in the abyssal language (he is fluent in common as well and listens intently to the characters). If they can communicate, Dun tells his story (see below). If none of the characters can speak with animals or speak Abyssal, Dun maintains his bat form. If the characters free him from the cage, he tries to get outside (through a chimney) where he can devise a new plot to lure the characters.

Dun Rathmon, Quasit: HD 3; HP 18; AC 2[17]; **Atk** 2 claws (1d2 + non-lethal poison), bite (1d3); **Move** 14; **Save** 14; **AL** C; **CL/XP** 7/600; **Special:** magic resistance (25%), non-lethal poison (save or weakened, −2 to hit and damage for 2d6 rounds), regenerate (1hp/ round), spell-like abilities. (*Monstrosities* 103)

Spell-like abilities: at will—*invisibility*, *polymorph self*; 1/day—*fear*.

Cinematic Element. Dun Rathmon, in addition to being a demon tasked with stealing souls, is a consummate actor. He is an engaging little cur, and given a few moments of conversation, he generally persuades others to his way of thinking. He's also very personable and should be played as an appropriate peer to the characters; he's not a sniveling wretch, and he's not an egotistical maniac. Dun is a cold, calculating predator with ages of experience.

Dun's Story: According to Dun, he was the familiar of an evil person by the name of Lassiter D'Torrance, a follower of the Demon-Princess Teratashia. D'Torrance was killed by a visitor named Torad Yarog, who took D'Torrance's place. This Torad Yarog is a murderer, and Dun can help the characters find him. Dun's motive is revenge and survival (neither of which is really untrue).

Dun is a potential source of information for the characters if they can convince the quasit that (a) they aren't going to kill him, and (b) that he has some advantage to working with them. If the characters treat him fairly — and he is very hard to fool — they might get various information about the following (not necessarily all at once)!

- **Teratashia:** The quasit is not directly in Teratashia's service, so he does not owe any loyalty to the demon-princess. However, he is very careful what information he divulges, simply out of fear.
- **Demon Ships:** The quasit knows that Teratashia sends minions through the gaps between the planes, and might offhandedly mention that sometimes these are ships. He does not specifically know that Torad Yarog has one of these ships in port or that he is the captain of one.
- **Lassiter:** Lassiter D'Torrance is dead, killed by Torad Yarog
- **Yarog:** Torad Yarog is a doppelganger. The quasit does not mention this at the outset, preferring to trade the information for advantage later on. If it appears that Dun would gain some benefit from giving the characters this piece of information, he does so.

TW41-25. Basement

This is a small underground room accessible from the staircase in the sunroom (**Area TW41-14**). This cold, damp room is lightless. If characters are able to see, they look upon a horrific nightmare. Chains and manacles are fastened to the walls, with bloody outlines suggesting someone has recently been hung down here. Bloody, putrid straw is piled up in the northwest corner, used to clean up some of the horrid mess. The smell of offal is thick, and the stench gets stronger as characters move east toward the marble wall.

Claustrophobic? The ceiling here is only seven feet tall, giving a very close, *heavy* feeling. The *weight* of the house, and all the horrors in the upper floors, as well as the influence of the Between requires all characters in the basement to make a saving throw. If successful, the characters are free to act normally. If the save fails, the character gains 1 level of mental exhaustion from the inundation of *burden*.

What Happened Here? This is where the Fiend grew bored with torture and mutilation and moved on to killing. The last of the doppelganger's initial playthings perished here a few weeks ago, but the vengeful spirits did not rest. Hidden under the pile of straw are **2 zombies**. The two wretches are former members of the Beggars Guild, suggesting the timeline for the killings began several weeks ago.

Zombies (2): HD 2; **HP** 14, 10; **AC** 8[11]; **Atk** strike (1d8); **Move** 6; **Save** 16; **AL** N; **CL/XP** 2/30; **Special:** immune to sleep and charm. (***Monstrosities*** 529)

Cinematic Element. This area should be presented as overwhelming in its grotesqueness. It is the initial efforts of a student of pain and suffering. It's not the place of this book to describe the atmosphere in detail (that's for you!), but describe it in terms your players will understand. This should be portrayed as an amateur's attempt at a grand gesture, but without the necessary skills. The gore in this room is representative of unbridled fury, engulfing rage, and crushing misery. There is no finesse to any of the wounds on the zombies, only blunt contusions and strength.

Eventually, a plan formed in the Fiend's jungle of a mind, and with the plan came focus. Such powerful, obsessive focus …

Mental Exhaustion. This place is disgusting, disturbing, and exaggeratedly gross. It is violently bloody for gore's sake. Characters entering the basement and observing the mess must make a saving throw or suffer 2 levels of mental exhaustion. Characters who failed their save against the claustrophobic effect earlier make this save with a −1 penalty.

TW41-25A. Crypt

This large marble bank of drawers is a crypt. Covering the entire east wall, this marble edifice is coated in dried blood, offal, and other less-identifiable matter. Bronze plaques are inset into the face of each of the nine drawers. The plaques once had writing or names engraved on them, but this has been scratched off and ruined. There are no handles or other protrusions of any kind.

Beyond the Wall. If characters investigate the wall for more than one minute, the entire facade peels off like a wave to engulf them. The wall is a **mimic**, but one that developed a taste for the dead. The creature attacks until a target stops fighting, then it moves on to another. It wishes to "age" its food before it consumes it. It has been feeding on the dozens of former torture victims for more than a month.

Mimic: HD 7; **HP** 47; **AC** 6[13]; **Atk** smash (2d6); **Move** 2; **Save** 9; **AL** N; **CL/XP** 8/800; **Special:** glue (save or stuck to mimic), mimicry (disguise as various items). (***Monstrosities*** 329)

The Restful Dead. Once the mimic is dealt with, characters can investigate the actual crypt. A much less ornate affair, the wall is made of stackstone, and the "doors" are simple wooden planks. The planks are easily removed and bear no names or markings. Each of the nine simple compartments houses a single corpse. Most of these bodies are unremarkable, each being minor members of the extended D'Torrance family.

However, one body is very important. One corpse, entombed in the top right compartment, possesses an ornate necklace. If removed and cleaned of filth, characters learn there is an engraving on the back. The body is the real Lassiter D'Torrance, dead now for at least two weeks. But how can this be if he is the supposed killer?

Treasure. The ornate necklace is worth 250 gp, and the back is engraved with the name "*L. D'Torrance.*"

TW41-25B. Vault

One of the compartments seems more solid than the others. This compartment is a false front to a hidden vault. Characters have a 1-in-6 chance to notice a gap around the plaque that can be depressed. Activating the switch causes the door to pop open and reveal a two-foot-tall pile of documents, ledgers, manifests, and other bundles of correspondence.

Treasure. The vault of Gaunt House contains many clues to the web of intrigue involved in the Fiend's grand plan. It also houses secret information that may change the balance of the entire adventure, so you are cautioned to consider everything being included. If Dun Rathmon is with the party, he is visibly excited when the characters open the vault.

The Tangled Web. As the characters rifle through the papers accumulated in the vault, they find a few special items:

- A shipping manifest from a ship called *The Shifting Fortune*. The ship is moored in Bard's Gate. The manifest looks ordinary, but upon inspection it does not make sense; the numbers and cargo are quite random.
- A ledger detailing business expenses for the D'Miean family, including several expenses for guilds in Castorhage, Reme, Bard's Gate, Courghais, and Freegate.
- Several stacks of handwritten notes detailing long-forgotten religious rites of various demons.

The Secret Digest. A small digest is hidden behind a secret panel in the cubby. Bound in a dull leather cover, the book is a treatise on the worship of the Demon-Princess Teratashia. The book is written in abyssal, but copious notes in deep speech are written in the margins, so a character able to speak either language can decipher the contents.

If the character finishes the digest, the end notes contain a magical secret: *The Secret of the Liar.* Information about the secret is detailed in **Appendix C: Written Secrets**.

Appendix A: New Monster

Cadaver

Hit Dice: 2
Armor Class: 6[13]
Attacks: 2 claws (1d4 + disease), bite (1d6 + disease)
Saving Throw: 16
Special: Disease, reincarnation
Move: 6
Alignment: Chaos
Number Encountered: 1, 1d6+2
Challenge Level: 4/120

Cadavers are humanoids dressed in tattered rags. Rotted flesh reveals corded muscles and sinew stretched tightly over its skeleton. Hollow eye sockets flicker with an unholy fire of orange or yellow light. The cadaver's mouth is lined with jagged and broken teeth, and its hands end in wicked claws. The creature's claws and bite transmit horrible diseases that waste victims' flesh (1d4 hit points damage; save resists). When killed, a cadaver regenerates 1 hit point per round. It stands up ready to fight again when it regains its full hit points. Damage caused by spells is not restored.

Cadaver: HD 2; AC 6[13]; Atk 2 claws (1d4 + disease), bite (1d6 + disease); Move 6; Save 16; AL C; CL/XP 4/120; **Special:** disease (wasting, 1d4 damage, save resists), reincarnation (regain 1hp per round until restored).

Appendix B: New Items

Equipment

Stink Pot (Pot of Stink)

This is a jar of condensed filth, comprising various bits of bodily excretions, secretions, sweat, funk, and general nonliving ooze. The stink is quite nauseating, and requires a save to avoid vomiting instantly, and retching violently for 1d6 rounds (–2 to hit and damage). Even with a successful save, the sniffer is rendered dizzy for one round and only able to defend themselves from attack (no attacks possible). The pot of stink is the "secret" secret weapon of the beggar who wants to make good his escape, and is in the possession of most journeymen and master beggars. Even once the stink has been overcome by its victim the stench remains. Clothes or armor touched by its stench must be administered a chemical or magical cleaning to remove the odor. Failure to remove the odor double the chance of random monster encounter until the stench has been dealt with. Members of the Beggars Guild, and denizens of the more fetid swamps and sewers are immune to the effects of a pot of stink.

Medium Miscellaneous Magical Item

Envoy's Signet

These dual-purpose items serve as a distinct signet ring — and one that heats wax to seal confidential correspondence — and hides the wearer from detection. The wearer cannot be targeted by magic to reveal their location, and area-of-effect spells do not function on the wearer.

Appendix C: Written Secrets

Written secrets may be found anywhere, but as such knowledge is powerful, it is usually hidden in code in the pages of an innocent book, scrawled in the margins of a spellbook in almost invisible writing, or subtly worked into art, poems, or other more obscure media. The discovery of secrets is left to you to handle. Take care, however, as these secrets are extremely rare in Castorhage and almost unheard of elsewhere.

Written secrets come in many forms. Each is bound by a trigger that may be a complex ceremony, a spell, or another action (up to and including sacrifice). The secret also has a consequence if it is triggered. Finally, the secret has a reward; some rewards come at a small cost, while some are considerable. Where losses — of hit points, ability scores, or other effects are inflicted — these are recoverable only through the use of a *wish* or similarly powerful spell, or through time.

Secrets are meant to be used once by a character; multiple uses are, in general, impossible, although you may wish to consider a suitable punishment for those who attempt to use secrets more than once. Growing an extra, hideous head, being haunted by a disgusting demonic lover night after dark, or something similarly unpleasant are good examples.

The Secret of the Liar

This secret allows the bearer to speak words of honey that charm and beguile those who hear them.

Trigger Speaking the words of the secret aloud.
Consequence The character is drawn in by the lies they tell. When the character first triggers the secret, they must make a successful saving throw with a –4 penalty or suffer 1 point of wisdom loss, which can be restored only by a *restoration* or *wish* spell.
Reward The character can cast *suggestion* once per day.
originally appeared in **The Blight** by **Frog God Games**

Appendix D: Teratashia

Teratashia resembles a huge, female-headed cockroach with a feral visage, who wears a necklace of human skulls. She is the Demon-Princess of Dimensions and Gaps, and as such is one of the major powers in the Between.

Her dark palace is located in the depths of the Abyss — a nexus of countless gaps between dimensions, of tunnels worming their way deep into a multitude of other realities. From the center of this web of connections, Teratashia sends her minions creeping and slithering through the planes of existence to do her bidding. Her motives and methods are inscrutable, for the demon-princess seldom involves herself in the quarrels of the other great demons. She is far more interested in controlling the nooks and crannies between dimensions than with her political status in the Abyss. She is inclined to leave the other demon princes alone to the same degree that they extend that courtesy to her.

THE LYRE VALLEY BEHOLDER

Bard's Gate	Manesdag, Freyrmond 5, 3518IR	2 penny

Rash of Missing Concerns Guild

This week, the Honorable Lucius Gromp again made his displeasure known to the city council over the disappearance of several local guildmembers. Citing a lack of resources to locate the missing, Gm Gromp was heard to say, "If the Beggers are no longer tolerated in the city, I can make preparations to leave," which drew an immediate vote by the council. A motion was proposed by none other than Gm Duloth Armitage, who said "If we cannot accept the lowest in our city, we hardly deserve the city itself."

A proposal to divert funds from the Outer Quarter constables' operating budget to create a "reward fund" was met with some resistance. The constables, quite understandably, have been hampered by last year's investigations into the "clown-faced kidnapper," and have been attempting to recoup costs and stabilize the district since. Unexpected aid from Maiden's Cross, in the form of funds and extra patrols, have helped significantly. The district owes the paladins of that fine establishment a debt of gratitude.

A formal vote on diverting funds is scheduled for the next council meeting; however, several businesses local to Turlin's Well and the Outer Quarter are pledging their own funds to finance an investigation. We here at the *Beholder* promise to keep you up-to-date on the developments of this story.

Return of the Fiend?

Noted district vandal "The Fiend" has another example of his vandalistic art on display, this time just south of Vok's on Nelson Way. The illustration is in the typical style: unexplainable, talented, but vandalism nonetheless. The Well Watch is still offering a 10 gp reward for information leading to the detainment of "The Fiend."

Solsdag 16 Special Event!

This Solsdag 16, eleven days from today marks the 101st anniversary of the construction of King's Bridge. All merchants of the Bridge District are offering special "King's Bridge Anniversary" deals, and many eateries are creating one-of-a-kind delicacies to promote the event. Festivities begin at sunrise on Solsdag and are scheduled to end after midnight.

A contest is scheduled for the children participating in the day: Collect all eight of the "personalities of Bard's Gate" tokens and receive a King's Bridge commemorative carved figurine from the Temple of Skilled Hands! Sure to be a fantastic collectible! Come early, stay late, and enjoy the 101st anniversary of the great King's Bridge!

Spring at the Sisters!

In addition to the festivities planned in the Bridge District, the notoriously raucous Wicked Sisters Café is offering a "Spring is Here" Sistersdag brunch special. Noted for their family-friendly brunches, bring the kids and sample some of the best home cooking in the city. Brunch plates start at 3 wheels each, a child's plate is 2 wheels, and children under 6 years eat for free! Come join in the festivities, and sisters Ewa and Tessa promise "You won't be disappointed!"

EYES ON THE CITY

Freyrmond 5–9
Fearsome Intent
Noted percussionists Torluk Von Trund and newcomer M'gok reunite as Fearsome Intent for four nights this spring. Tickets are still available for all shows except Freyrmond 8 (sold out). Tickets are available at the door or from the Thunder Hall front office. *The Masque and Lute*

Freyrmond 6
Wonkee Gallery Showing
Beholder staff artist "Wonkee" has a gallery showing at the Feng bathhouse Sistersdag 6. Show begins at dusk. In keeping with his eclectic nature, this is an adults-only showing, and refreshments will be available. *Dreams of Feng*

Freyrmond 15
Words of the World
World-renowned traveler and bard JD Mekson talks about her travels on and off the common roads in this two-hour symposium. She describes the cultural currents of the times, political insight, and brings news from the western coast. A city favorite, please welcome JD for her one-night stand! *The Clarion Call, shop floor*

Freyrmond 23
Hartine Russe
Hadran's Dome is pleased to welcome Hartine Russe back for ONE NIGHT ONLY! Hartine has been on a continental tour of Waymarch and makes a triumphant return to the Dome. Special VIP seating is available, and a meet-and-great is scheduled for the afternoon before the performance. Limited seating still available! *Hadran's Dome*

Freyrmond 24-30
Umberto Deleon Gallery
Extraordinary painter Umberto Deleon is having an "open house" gallery at his studio in the college district. Come see how the master works, from Freyrmond 24–30. Doors are open from just after highnoon to dusk. Entrance is FREE! *Umberto's Studio*

MASTER SCULPTOR, UTELLO

One of the most prominent artists of the city and this age, Utello's ornamentation graces many of the great temples and lofty homes in the Hill district. Utello's gargoyles are highly sought-after pieces of art and architecture, commanding thousands of harps for even a small representation. (This reporter is fortunate enough to have a small Utello "guarding" his own doorstep at home.) A former apprentice to the artist Phidian, Utello has taken his former teacher's work to a greater extreme. An artist of great skill and patience, it is our honor to sit with this master in his Turlin's Well studio for this interview.

Good morning sir! I must get one thing out in the open right off: I am a HUGE fan of your work! I have one of your smaller pieces at my own home, and I must say, in the right lighting, its eyes DO seem to follow me!

(Heh) Well, I appreciate the thanks. It's always nice to hear from an appreciative customer. I do get quite a bit of sour looks from me work, you know. General folks don' like to look at the dark, now, do they?

People don't like your work? It's everywhere, it's almost a mainstay of the architectural flavor of the city …

Like I said, people don' like to look at their dark nature. That's why my art is so black or white; I can see what lies in people's souls. (slaps his knee) HAW! Got ye with that one! Should have caught the look on yer face! Helps the persona if I seem all dark and menacing. Nobody wants to buy a gargoyle from a happy guy. They expect it to come from some dark witch-queen in some twisted tower, and that the thing could come to life at any instant and pull yer heart from your body. THAT'S the story people are looking for. The backstory, the terror that shows them what they deal with day to day ain' the horror of the world.

I'm convinced. You did have me for a second.

These things are just stone. Stone, time, and sweat. Maybe some inspiration, maybe some inner demons, but that's it. Nothing to really be afraid of. (He winks as he says this. I am unsure how I feel about this interview at this moment. Something is tingling the hairs on my neck)

(He interrupts me composing myself)

Now, that vandal down in the streets, what do they call him, "the friend"? Or the "fiend," or something like that? That one has a problem. His art, his graffiti, it ain' art. It's a message. I jus' can't figure out to who, or to what.

Do you know who the Fiend is?

Naw, don' want to either. I'll just stay in here with my friends and let that sort itself out.

Understood. Well, can I get to the standard questions? Seems like we've run short on time a bit. Favorite meal in Bard's Gate?

Right to it then? Fair off. Favorite meal is probably any of those patrons that don' pay off after a special piece they order. I like to roast over a low fire, maybe say a few chants … (winks)

You have to stop doing that!

Heh, son, you can't change your nature. I'm a villain at heart, I jus' don't practice.

Do you have a favorite local bar?

Good recovery. I don' mind the 'Rose; got a nice view in there. I like the food at Rising Dragon; different, spicy, got some flavor the rest of the city is missing. It's good.

Immediate opening for a highly motivated, honest, dependable Painter's Helper.
Must be very experienced in residential repaints. Must be drug and alcohol free. Must have own tools and be local to the Guild district. Full Time Position. Paid weekly. Apply at 24 Lower Cristofferson Dr. Ask for Micha.

POSITION: Inventory/Warehouse Helper for the Wheelwrights Guild
Status: Temporary
Location: Guild district
Department: Materials

SUMMARY: This position is responsible for assisting Warehouse Associates with packing, receiving, and stocking of materials. The position reports to the Inventory Storage & Distribution Manager or designee.

ESSENTIAL DUTIES AND RESPONSIBILITIES: Assist with receiving, shipping, and stockroom duties. Assist with part-scrapping project. Adhere to all safety and security policies and regulations. Report to work on a regular and consistent basis.

REQUIRED ABILITY TO: Accurately pull and organize materials. Physically lift, move, push and pull up to fifty (50) pounds on a consistent basis. Demonstrate good verbal and written communication skills. Build alliances, partnerships and collaborate with co-workers in a tactful, professional and respectful manner. Be a team player with strong interpersonal skills. Resolve workplace differences and conflict to achieve goals and objectives in a professional manner. Listen to others attentively and retain/process information effectively. Promote a professional culture that is trustworthy, honest, and socially responsible while championing an energetic and positive work culture.

WORKING CONDITIONS: Continuous walking and standing, and lifting, pushing and pulling heavy objects throughout the workday. Continuous exposure to outdoor elements. Flexibility to work long hours and occasional weekends.

The Wheelwrights are an Equal Opportunity Employer and do not unlawfully discriminate on the basis of race, sex, age, color, sexual orientation, religion, national origin, marital status, genetic information, veteran's status, disability or any other basis prohibited by local law.

The Wheelwrights provide reasonable accommodation to its employees and the public with disabilities, including disabled veterans. For more information, including salaries and full job description, please visit the Wheelwrights Guild, Guildhall Ct.

Interested in active work and have a background in landscaping or moving?
There are many opportunities on the westside that are looking for General Labor support!
Positions are available in a variety of fields such as moving, sorting materials, warehouses, and window installation. Temporary and temp-to-hire opportunities available!

General Labor Responsibilities:
- Load/unload individual items on dollies and carts.
- Sorting/Stocking items.
- Some light delivery service.

No specific experience is required for any of these roles, but a background in landscaping, warehouse, or furniture moving is a plus!

Requirements: Ability to lift 60–100 pounds throughout shift

Pay: Ranges from 1–3 sw/day depending on position and experience

Schedule: Specific schedules differ for each role.
Some companies offer benefits, including housing coverage

Location: Varies per position, available jobs are in the Market, Guild, or Old Temple districts.
- Depending on the location and shift availability, a cart may or may not be required.
Interested in these General Labor opportunities? Apply today!

ARTIST SEEKS LIFE MODEL: Collegiate painter seeks model inspiration. Looking for the new and different/complete beginners are fine. Need several new models who are unique, unafraid, and open to guidance. Apply at Waterfront 3, plaza of dark pleasures. Compensation based on negotiated contract.

SEEKING: Longshoremen. All shifts, all days. Experience preferred, but will train right person. 1 drum per day, 3 drums for experienced dock hands. Inquire at the Tradeway Landing offices off South Badalato St. Malik Truock is the contact.

CARPENTERS WANTED: We have openings for new and experienced carpenters. Are you just starting out, no tools or experience, but willing to work hard and learn? We will pay you 2 silver wheels/day to learn. From there we pay more based on ability, up to 10 sw/day. Must be a team player, work well with others, show up to work ready to work, and enjoy the process of building. Please deliver references to Landmark Job Office, 6 Hersh-Grohe Rd., Guild district, for an interview. Immediate openings available.

Vinewood Winery Seeks Transporters

The world-renowned Vinewood Winery is seeking transporters for the upcoming spring seasonals. Several vintages will be ready for the Eostre festivals, and Vinewood NEEDS YOU! Your wagon, your team, our product. Price is one silver wheel per barrel delivered, half paid up front. Collateral required, references REQUIRED. Background checks run on all applicants.

Security detail required, paid for by applicant. Proof of detail required.

Apply at the Inn of Six Candles. Seek Charles, who will give further details.

FROG GOD
GAMES
ADVENTURES
WORTH WINNING